grk

SMELLS A RAT!

grk

SMELLS A RAT!

Josh Lacey

Andersen Press · London

First published in 2008 by
Andersen Press Limited,
20 Vauxhall Bridge Road, London SWIV 2SA
www.andersenpress.co.uk

This edition published in 2013

British Library Cataloguing in Publication Data available

ISBN 978 1 84939 738 4

Mixed Sources
Product group from well-managed
forests and other controlled sources
www.fsc.org Cert no. TT-COC-0002227
© 1996 Forest Stewardship Council
FSC

Typeset by FiSH Books, Enfield, Middx.
Printed and bound in Great Britain by CPI Group (UK)
Ltd, Croydon, CR0 4YY

Chapter 1

If you were a millionaire, what would you buy?

Yes, of course, you'd buy a house. And then another house. And then a few more houses.

You'd probably buy some cars too. Maybe a couple of planes and helicopters. And a few boats.

But what would you buy next?

A football team? An island? A space station?

If you were so rich that money meant nothing to you, how would you spend your millions?

Vijay Ghat was one of the richest men in India. He had made millions and millions and millions of rupees by gambling on the stock market. He'd made millions of dollars, pounds, yen and euros too.

He employed hundreds of servants, dozens of advisers and an army of highly trained, heavily armed bodyguards.

He owned eleven houses, twenty-eight cars, three planes, two helicopters, twelve boats, two islands and a cricket team. (He didn't like football.)

Although Vijay Ghat didn't yet have his own personal space station, he had employed a group of seventy scientists to build him a rocket and he was intending to fly to the moon as soon as he could.

And he still had masses of money to spare.

So he had decided to buy himself a tennis tournament.

He hired the New Delhi Lawn Tennis Club for a fortnight, booked every room in one of Delhi's finest hotels and paid for some of the world's best young players to fly to India.

Because he wanted everyone to know who had paid for everything, he named the tournament after himself.

Tonight, there was a party to celebrate the opening of the Vijay Ghat International Lawn Tennis Association Under-Sixteen Championship.

All competitors were expected to attend. Their families and coaches were invited too.

A long queue of limousines drove through the tall front gates of Vijay Ghat's immense mansion and dropped guests at the entrance. Valets darted forwards, opened the door of each limousine and ushered the guests onto the long red carpet which led to the front door. There, more servants were waiting, taking the names of guests, making sure no one came inside who hadn't been invited.

TV cameras recorded footage which would be broadcast later on the evening news. Photographers snapped pictures for tomorrow's papers. Journalists scribbled notes in their notebooks, recording the details of who attended the party and what they were wearing.

As a big black Mercedes rolled to a halt, a valet darted forward. Cameras swivelled. Microphones were raised. Pens hovered over the pages of notebooks. The journalists waited to see which celebrity was going to emerge.

The valet opened the door of the Mercedes. Immediately, a dog jumped out of the car and landed on the red carpet.

It was a small dog with black eyes. It had white fur with black patches and a perky little tail.

As soon as its four feet landed on the carpet, the dog turned its head from side to side and sniffed the air, as if it could smell something quite fascinating, not very far away.

The journalists turned to one another, asking all kinds of questions. 'Who is this dog?' said one of them.

'What is he doing here?' said another.

'Why has he been invited?' said a third.

'Does Vijay know him?'

'Is he famous?'

'Does he belong to someone famous?'

'What's so important about him?'

The dog was followed by a boy, who was holding the dog's lead. The boy was followed by another boy, then a girl and then two adults.

When the journalists saw all these people, they immediately lost interest. The journalists could see immediately that not one of them was remotely famous or important. And nor was their dog. Therefore, they were not interesting to the people who watched the evening news or bought a morning newspaper. All the journalists turned their attention to the next limousine in the queue, wondering who was going to emerge from that one, hoping it would be someone really famous. A politician, perhaps. Or a pop star. Or an actress. Someone whose face would be recognised by everyone who lived in India and whom everyone would want to see on the front page of tomorrow's papers.

Grk, Tim, Max, Natascha and the Malts walked past the pack of journalists and headed for the front door of Vijay Ghat's mansion.

Any of them could have told the journalists that there was one very simple reason why they were here. Not because they were famous. Nor because they were important. No, the reason was this: Max Raffifi had been invited to take part in the Vijay Ghat International Lawn Tennis Association Under-Sixteen Championship and the others had come to support him.

When the Malts and the Raffifis had walked down the carpet, past the servants, through the front door, along the hallway and into the ballroom, they stopped and stood still, speechless with astonishment, not knowing what to say or think.

That's what the Malts and the Raffifis did, anyway. Grk was different. He knew exactly what to do and precisely where he wanted to go. He didn't care about the gold furniture or the elegant paintings. He wasn't interested in the expensive clothes worn by other guests or even their fancy haircuts. He just wanted to run across the room as fast as his little legs would carry him, leap into the air and land on top of one of the tables piled high with food. There, he'd be happy to spend the rest of his life, or at least the rest of the night, eating his way through the stacks of curried chicken and grilled lamb and raw fish that he had been able to

4

smell since the moment that he stepped out of the limousine.

Unfortunately, he couldn't go anywhere, because he had a collar clasped around his neck. There was a lead attached to his collar and Tim was holding the other end of the lead.

Oh, well. You're allowed to dream, aren't you? Even if you're a small dog on a tight lead. Grk lifted his nose into the air and took long, deep sniffs of all the different delicious scents that were floating around the room.

While Grk was smelling all the food, the Malts and the Raffifis were staring open-mouthed at the most exclusive, expensive and extraordinary party that any of them had ever attended.

The high-ceilinged room was packed with guests and servants. Politicians chatted to pop stars. Industrialists gossiped with actors. Skinny, beautiful women clung to the arms of bald, fat millionaires.

Along the walls, wooden tables creaked under the weight of the vast quantities of food. There were samosas, pakoras, kebabs, idlis and dosas, and every imaginable variety of curry. Great pyramids of rice, flavoured and coloured with saffron, were heaped on huge silver platters alongside little bowls of pickle and chutney. If you didn't like Indian food, you could choose sushi, spaghetti, hamburgers, hot dogs or a hundred different dishes from all around the world.

At one end of the room there was a wooden platform with a microphone on a stand, ready for someone to come and make a speech.

At the other end of the room there was an enormous fountain, which had been built especially for the party. Sprays of brown liquid shot into the air and gurgled down the sides, collecting in a great wide bowl at the bottom. Most fountains flow with water, but this one gushed an unending stream of pure warm chocolate.

Some guests dipped strawberries into the flowing chocolate. Others preferred pineapple chunks or mango slices. The greediest just filled champagne glasses and drank down great gulps of liquid chocolate.

Chapter 2

Staring at millionaires soon gets boring. That's what Tim thought, anyway. He didn't want to talk to them, listen to them or even look at them. He would have been much happier lying in bed, reading a book or watching TV.

To his surprise, the others didn't appear to share his feelings.

Mr Malt was engaged in an animated conversation with a red-faced billionaire, discussing what was wrong with English cricketers and what they could learn from the Indian national team. Mrs Malt was swapping stock market tips with a group of Indian businesswomen. Max was discussing weather conditions with three other tennis players. Only Natascha wasn't involved in a conversation, but she looked perfectly happy to be here: she was wandering through the party with her notebook, jotting down scraps of information and gossip that she overheard. If she'd been an adult, people would have assumed she was a journalist and stopped talking as soon as they saw her, but no one took any notice of a girl.

Even Grk seemed to be happy. He put his nose into the air and sniffed all the extraordinary smells that were filtering through the room, dreaming about the delicious foods that he could have been eating – if only he could slip off his collar and roam freely through the party.

Tim tried to pass the time by eating as much chocolate as possible, but even that wasn't much fun. After two glasses of pure liquid chocolate, six slices of chocolate-covered mango and eleven chunks of chocolate-covered pineapple, he felt quite sick.

Suddenly, a voice shouted across the room, 'Silence! Silence, please! Pray be silent for your host, Vijay Ghat!'

The room went quiet.

Everyone stopped their conversations and turned to face the wooden platform at the end of the room.

Tim popped one final piece of chocolate-covered pineapple into his mouth and wiped the stray chocolate from his lips, then turned to face the platform too.

A small man was standing at the front of the platform, holding a microphone. He was wearing an immaculate black suit, a white shirt and a blue silk tie. With his perfectly polished nails and well-groomed black hair, he looked as if he had never come into contact with dirt.

He leaned forward and spoke into a microphone. 'My name is Vijay Ghat,' he said. 'Welcome to my home.'

He clasped his hand together, palms touching, and made a slight bow. In return, many of his guests did exactly the same gesture back to him.

As you probably know, this gesture is called a *namaste*. It's the way that people greet one another in India.

'Some of you have come from elsewhere in Delhi to be here tonight,' said Vijay Ghat. 'Others have come from Mumbai, Kolkata and other Indian cities. And yet more of you have travelled many thousands of miles from all around the world. I would like to thank you for making such an effort to be here. Welcome! Welcome, all of you! Welcome to India, to Delhi and to my house!'

There was a ripple of polite applause from the assembled guests. When Tim noticed that everyone else was clapping, he clapped too, although he wasn't sure what he was supposed to be clapping about.

Vijay Ghat held up his hands for silence. 'There is something else that I must say. Something much more important. I want to welcome you not just to my humble home, but to the first Vijay Ghat International Lawn Tennis Association Under-Sixteen Championship.'

This time, the applause was louder and more enthusiastic. At the back of the room, people cheered and whistled.

'Tennis has always been my favourite game,' said Vijay Ghat with a broad smile. 'It is the purest of all games. One man against one man. One woman against one woman. One individual against one individual. All around the world, people love tennis. People play tennis. And people compete in tennis tournaments. You are probably wondering to yourself why I have decided to sponsor another tennis tournament. Aren't there enough already? Does the world really need another?'

Vijay Ghat paused and looked around the room as if he was expecting someone to answer his questions. Of course, no one did. He let the silence continue for a few seconds, then answered his own question himself. 'The

Vijay Ghat International Lawn Tennis Association Under-Sixteen Championship is a tournament concerned entirely with the future. The only players who can enter this tournament are the players of the future. Our children. The children of the world. A few years from now, the world will belong to them. This tournament is their chance to show us what they can do. I am delighted that so many young players have entered the tournament from all around the world and so many of you are here tonight in my humble home. Please, a round of applause for the players!'

This time, Vijay Ghat started the clapping and all his guests followed. Then he held up his hands for silence.

'Now, you have heard enough of my voice. The day after tomorrow, I shall see you at the first match of the Vijay Ghat International Lawn Tennis Association Under-Sixteen Championship. But now let's enjoy ourselves. Eat. Drink. Make merry. Enjoy the party!'

To the accompaniment of loud applause, Vijay Ghat switched off the microphone, stepped down from the platform and started walking through the crowd, meeting his guests. People stepped forward to shake his hand and thank him for his wonderful hospitality.

Wherever he went, Vijay Ghat was surrounded by eight bodyguards, three photographers and four advisers, two on either side, who took turns to speak quietly into his ears, informing him exactly who he was meeting, what they were called, where they came from and why they had been invited to this party. Using this information, Vijay Ghat was always able to ask the right questions of the right people as if he knew all about them himself.

Vijay Ghat had been walking around the party for more than an hour, accompanied by his crowd of bodyguards, photographers and advisers, when he reached a small group of people standing in a corner of the ballroom: two adults, three children and a dog.

One of the advisers leaned forward and put his mouth close to Vijay Ghat's ear. 'The boy on the left is Max Raffifi,' whispered the adviser. 'A very good player. He won gold medals in Argentina and New Zealand. Most recently, he won the Bethnal Green Challenge Cup. He has a good chance of winning the championship.'

Armed with this information, Vijay Ghat started talking to Max. 'Welcome to my house, Mr Raffifi,' he said. 'I'm so glad that you're here. It is a great pleasure to meet you! I hope you'll have great success in my tournament, just as you did in Argentina, New Zealand and Bethnal Green.'

'Thank you very much,' said Max. 'I hope so too.'

Another of Vijay Ghat's advisers whispered in his other ear. Immediately, Vijay Ghat turned around and focused his attention on another of the children. 'Hello, my young friend,' he said. 'You must be Timothy Malt.'

'That's right,' said Tim. 'I am.'

'I hear you've had great success defeating those wicked Pelotti brothers in Brazil. And this must be your dog, Grk. Am I right?'

Tim nodded, very surprised that Vijay Ghat knew so much about him and his family – and their dog too.

11

'Hello, Grk,' said Vijay Ghat.

Hearing his name, Grk wagged his tail.

Vijay Ghat said, 'A great pleasure to meet you, Tim, and you too, Grk. And all the rest of you. Have a wonderful evening.' He turned to Max and said, 'Good luck, Max. I hope to see you at the tournament – and I hope you have great success in your games.' With that, Vijay Ghat was gone, moving onwards through the crowd, meeting and greeting more of his guests.

'What a charming man,' said Mrs Malt.

'Not just charming,' said Mr Malt. 'Brilliant, too. He's one of the cleverest and most successful businessmen in the whole of India. He's worth billions. He must be one of the richest men in the world.'

Chapter 3

As you will know if you have read *A Dog Called Grk*, Max Raffifi was one of the world's best young tennis players. He won gold medals in the New Zealand Under-Sixteen Lawn Tennis Cup and the Argentinian Teenage Tennis Open Finals.

After the death of his parents, Max lost interest in games. Batting a ball around a court, counting up the points, trying to beat other people – he couldn't imagine anything so ridiculous. Compared to the murders of his father and mother, tennis seemed trivial.

One day, Mrs Malt suggested to her husband that they should buy him a tennis racket. 'Max takes everything so seriously,' she said. 'Playing a game might be good for him.'

'He has a very good reason for taking things so seriously,' her husband replied.

'But he's only fifteen. You can't carry the woes of the world on your shoulders when you're only fifteen.'

Mr Malt shrugged his shoulders. 'There's no reason not to try, I suppose. But I'll be amazed if he ever plays.'

The following weekend, Mrs Malt took Max to a sports shop and bought him a racket, some shoes, some white shorts and a couple of white shirts. There was a tennis club near the house. Mrs Malt bought Max a six-month membership. 'If you never play,' she said, 'we won't bother renewing it. But you've got six months to decide.'

For several weeks, Max didn't even go to the club. He always found something better to do. And then, one Saturday morning, without telling anyone where he was going, he changed into his tennis clothes, picked up his racket and wandered down there. He sat beside the courts, watching other people play.

After an hour or two, someone challenged him to a game. Max shrugged his shoulders and said, 'Sure, why not?'

Max hadn't played for a long time. He lost the first point. And the second point. And the third, fourth and fifth.

His arms ached. His legs too. He was tempted to give up and go home. But he forced himself to run from one side of the court to the other, chasing every ball. Gradually, his body seemed to remember how to play tennis. He started winning every point.

He went back the next Saturday. And the Saturday after that. Soon, he was going to the tennis club every day of the week, practising for hours.

People started to find excuses not to play him. They didn't like being beaten. Max found himself without any opponents. That was when he started entering competitions.

He won the first competition that he entered. And the second. And then he won two more. Just as he was wondering which competition to enter next, he received an invitation to come to India and compete in the Vijay Ghat International Lawn Tennis Association Under-Sixteen Championship.

Chapter 4

Early in the morning, Tim, Natascha, Grk and the Malts left their hotel and took a taxi to New Delhi Railway Station.

The tennis tournament started tomorrow. In his first match, Max had been drawn against an Australian boy named Troy Crown. Today, Max was staying in the hotel, eating, sleeping and thinking through his tactics for tomorrow's game. Meanwhile, the others were taking the train from Delhi to Agra, where they were going to see one of the most famous buildings in the world.

Mr Malt always insisted on arriving at least half an hour early whenever he took public transport and twice that in a foreign country, but today he needn't have bothered. Forty minutes late, the train eased out of the station. Mr Malt glanced at his watch and shook his head, appalled by the delay.

Mr and Mrs Malt were very busy people. Mr Malt worked as an insurance underwriter. Mrs Malt worked as a financial consultant specialising in corporate takeovers. They both had to work extremely hard. They didn't have time to rush off to India, watch tennis tournaments, sit on trains or visit famous buildings.

Or rather, in the old days, they wouldn't have had time. But life has changed. Business has changed. Most importantly, communications have changed. Wherever you are in the world, you can now continue communicating with your bosses and your colleagues as if you're still sitting at your own desk in your own office.

That was why, as the train chugged through the Indian countryside, neither Mr nor Mrs Malt looked out of the window. They were too busy working. Both of them were hunched over their laptops, staring at the screen and typing quickly, writing reports which they would email back to their offices in London.

Natascha hardly glanced out of the window either. She was absorbed in reading a book called *The Story of My Experiments with Truth*. It was the autobiography of a wise man named Mahatma Gandhi. Every few pages, she scribbled some notes in the margin, wanting to record her thoughts about particular passages.

Tim had a book to read too, but he hadn't even opened it. He could read perfectly well at home. While he was here, he wanted to learn more about India and Indians and the way that people lived in this enormous, fascinating, complicated country. So he stared out of the window, watching the landscape thunder past, trying to notice all the ways in which India was different from home.

A man walked through the train, carrying a red bucket in one hand and a metal container in the other. The red bucket was packed with small clay pots.

'*Chai!*' the man called out. '*Chai! Chai! Chai!*'

As you probably know, hundreds of different languages are spoken throughout India, but most people

17

speak at least some English or Hindi. If you can speak one of those languages, you'll usually manage to find someone who can understand you.

Lots of words in Hindi and English are quite similar. '*Chai*', for instance, is almost the same word in both languages. Can you guess what it means?

Don't worry if you can't. Tim couldn't either. He had no idea what the man might be carrying in his metal container.

Here he came down the corridor, carrying his red bucket and his metal container, swaying in time with the movement of the train.

'*Chai!*' he shouted. '*Chai! Chai! Chai!*' He stopped beside Tim and said, 'You want *chai*?'

'I don't know,' said Tim, peering at the metal container. 'What's *chai*?'

'*Chai* is tea. You know tea?'

'Yes,' said Tim. 'I know tea. Well, I know what tea is, anyway.'

'You want tea?'

'How much does it cost?'

'One rupee.'

'Go on, then,' said Tim. He didn't really like tea, but he liked trying new things. More importantly, he wanted one of the little clay cups. They looked nice. He thought that one rupee was about one tenth of a penny, which seemed like a fair price for a nice small clay pot filled with tea, even if he chose to pour the tea out of the window.

The *chai*-seller put his bucket and his container on the

18

floor. The container had a small metal tap. That's where the tea came out.

But before the *chai*-seller could pour some tea into one of the small clay pots, Mrs Malt leaned forward and waggled her forefinger at him. 'No!' she said in a loud voice. 'No, thank you! We don't want to buy anything, thank you very much!'

Mrs Malt believed that the best way to communicate with foreigners was to speak slowly and loudly in clear English. In the three days since she arrived in India, this method had worked perfectly well, so she hadn't found any reason to change her beliefs.

The *chai*-seller looked disappointed. 'No tea?'

'No, thank you,' said Mrs Malt. 'We don't want to buy any tea or any coffee or anything else, thank you very much.'

The *chai*-seller gave Tim a sad glance as if to say, 'If you didn't want tea, why did you ask for tea?' Without giving Tim a chance to respond, he picked up his bucket and his container, and continued down the corridor, calling out to everyone in the carriage: '*Chai! Chai! Chai! Chai!*'

When the *chai*-seller's voice had faded, replaced by all the other noises of the train, Mrs Malt turned her attention to her son. She said, 'We've talked about this already, Tim. Haven't we?'

'Yes, Mum.'

'What did I tell you about food and drink?'

'You told me not to eat anything or drink anything.'

'That's not quite true, Tim. Is it?'

19

'No, Mum.'

'If you didn't eat anything or drink anything, you'd die, and you know perfectly well that I don't want you to die. Don't you?'

'Yes, Mum.'

'I just don't want you to get ill. So what did I actually say?'

'You said I should only drink bottled water,' said Tim. 'And you also said I should only eat food in clean restaurants after I'd washed my hands.'

'Exactly,' said Mrs Malt. 'Clean water and clean hands. Because we don't want to get diarrhoea, do we?'

'No, Mum.'

'If you're thirsty, have some bottled water.'

'I'm not thirsty.'

'Then why did you just try to buy a cup of tea?'

For a moment, Tim considered explaining that he had planned to tip the tea out of the window and keep the little clay cup, but decided not to bother. His mum wouldn't understand. She'd just give him a lecture about cleanliness or money or some other equally boring topic. So he didn't bother saying anything. Instead, he just shrugged his shoulders, slumped back in his seat and stared out of the window.

Chapter 5

A skinny boy walked down the corridor, swaying from side to side with the movement of the train, and stopped beside the Malts.

The boy was wearing dark trousers, a beige shirt and sandals. He must have been ten or eleven years old. He had black hair, gleaming white teeth and a wide smile. In his right hand, he was carrying a big plastic bag.

'Hello,' said the boy. 'Good morning. How are you?'

Without even looking up from her laptop, Mrs Malt said, 'We don't want to buy anything, thank you very much.'

'No problem,' said the boy. 'I am not selling anything at all. I am just here for the chitchat.'

'We don't want any of that either, thank you,' said Mrs Malt, her head bowed over her laptop, her fingers typing quickly, rattling the keys, spitting out sentence after sentence of her report.

'No problem,' said the boy. His smile seemed to get even wider. 'My name is Krishnan. I am very pleased to be meeting you. Please, tell me, where are you from?'

Neither Mr nor Mrs Malt bothered answering. They were too engrossed in what they were writing. Natascha lifted her head quickly and smiled at Krishnan, but didn't answer either, returning her attention immediately to the pages of her book. So Tim answered for all of them. He said, 'We live in England.'

'England?' Krishnan smiled. 'Very good country. Very good cricket, yes?'

'I suppose so,' said Tim. He wasn't terribly interested in cricket. He'd played a few times at school, but couldn't really see the point.

'Geoff Boycott, Graham Gooch, Andrew Flintoff. You know them?'

'No,' said Tim. 'I don't know them.'

'No problem,' said Krishnan. 'My name is Krishnan. And your name is, please?'

'Tim,' said Tim.

'Welcome to India, Mister Tim. Is this your first time in my country?'

'Yes.'

'You like India?'

'I'm not sure,' said Tim. 'I've only been here for a couple of days. I haven't had a chance to decide yet.'

'Let me tell you, Mister Tim, you will be happy here beyond your wildest dreams. You go now to Agra?'

'Yes.'

'You will see the Taj Mahal?'

'Yes.'

'Have you ever previously seen the Taj Mahal?'

'I've seen one place called the Taj Mahal,' said Tim. 'It's a restaurant near my house. They do delicious chicken korma.'

'No, no, the Taj Mahal is not a restaurant. The Taj Mahal is the most beautiful building in the world. I can tell you now, Mister Tim, you will be very happy to see the Taj Mahal. You will not believe your eyes.' Krishnan smiled. 'You want to buy one English book?'

'No, thanks,' said Tim. 'I've got enough books.'

'I have many good English books.' Krishnan opened his plastic bag. 'All good books. Many good English words. Fine paper. You want see one English book?'

'No, thanks,' said Tim. 'But you could ask her.' Tim pointed at Natascha. 'She always wants more books.'

Krishnan smiled at Natascha. 'Really? Yes? You would like to buy one good English book?'

'No, thanks,' said Natascha, hardly even lifting her head from the book that she was reading.

'You love books,' said Tim.

'I know I do,' said Natascha. 'But I've got enough.'

'You always say people could never have too many books,' said Tim. 'I've heard you say that a hundred times.'

Natascha sighed. She closed her book, putting her pen between the pages to mark her place, and looked at Krishnan. 'Go on, then. What have you got? What are you selling?'

'I have many good English books,' said Krishnan. 'I can supply whatever you wish. Big books. Small books. Funny books. Sad books. I can give you them all. Today, I have one fine copy of Harry Potter. You know Harry Potter?'

'Yes,' said Natascha. 'I've read all the Harry Potters.'

'Harry Potter is a very good magic boy.'

'Yes, I know,' said Natascha. 'I just told you, I've read them all.'

'Here, I have one very good Harry Potter book.' Krishnan reached into his bag and pulled out a copy of *Harry Potter and the Deathly Hallows*. 'You want to buy this most excellent book?'

'I told you, I've read it already. I've read them all.'

'But this is a very good price.'

'How much?'

'Three hundred rupees.' Krishnan smiled. 'Very good book, very cheap price.'

'Three hundred rupees,' said Natascha. 'What's that in English money?'

Without looking up from the screen of his laptop, Mr Malt said, 'About four pounds.'

'Gosh, that is cheap,' said Natascha, suddenly wavering. She took the book from Krishnan's hand and stared at the clean, smooth, unbroken spine. She could see immediately that this copy of *Harry Potter and the Deathly Hallows* was brand new and unread. It was a bargain. Natascha nodded at Krishnan. 'All right, I'll buy it.'

Krishnan was delighted. 'You are my first customer today,' he said. 'I am very, very happy.'

'I'm happy too,' said Natascha.

'You happy, me happy,' said Krishnan with a big smile. 'This is good. We are all happy.'

From her purse, Natascha counted out three hundred rupees in crumpled old notes. When they had arrived in India, Mr Malt had given her and Tim a thousand rupees each as pocket money. Until now, Natascha hadn't spent a single rupee.

'Thank you, thank you,' said Krishnan, taking the money and quickly counting the notes. Satisfied, he stuffed them into the pocket of his shirt and handed the book to Natascha. 'Please, you will enjoy this book very much.'

'Thanks,' said Natascha, opening the book and flicking through the first few pages.

Krishnan grinned at Tim. 'You want to buy one book?'

'No, thank you,' said Tim.

'Another time, maybe.'

'Maybe,' said Tim.

'Okey-dokey,' said Krishnan. 'Thank you for your customer. I hope you will have a most wonderful time in the Taj Mahal. Goodbye.'

Krishnan turned and walked away.

At that moment, Tim noticed something strange.

Behind Krishnan's right ear there was a little blue blotch. It looked a little bit like a wart, a birthmark or a stain.

Most people wouldn't have noticed anything unusual. And even if they had, they wouldn't have been very interested. If they'd happened to spot a blue blotch on the back of a boy's ear, they would simply have assumed that he hadn't washed himself properly. He'd been mucking around with a broken biro, they'd have said to themselves, or fallen asleep on a damp blue pillow.

But Tim had sharper eyesight than most people. He took a good long look at the small blueish blotch on the underside of the boy's ear and saw that it wasn't actually a wart, a birthmark or a stain, but a tiny, intricate tattoo of a rat.

A small blue rat with a long wriggly tail.

Tim was intrigued. He'd never seen a tattoo on the back of someone's ear before. He wondered why Krishnan had tattooed his ear with a blue rat and what it might mean. But there was no chance to find out. Before Tim could say anything, both Krishnan and his bag of books had gone into the next carriage.

Chapter 6

They sat in silence. Mr and Mrs Malt typed on their laptops. Natascha read her new book. Tim stared out of the window and took a photo whenever he saw something interesting. Grk lay on the floor at their feet, snoozing and dreaming.

Every few minutes, another salesman walked along the train, carrying a bag, a box or a tray filled with goods. They called out in English and Hindi, describing what they were selling. Some had grapes, bananas and mangoes. Others had packets of crisps and chewing gum or bottles of water and fruit juice. Yet more offered homemade snacks like vegetable samosas, pakoras and chapattis. One salesman even had a big bucket packed with orange ice lollies, melting in the heat.

Every one of these salesmen stopped beside the Malts and offered them a selection of their wares, trying to tempt Tim or Natascha into making a purchase, but Mrs Malt always shooed them away before they had a chance to utter more than a few words.

'You might as well save your breath,' she said in a stern voice. 'We're quite happy as we are, thank you. We don't want to buy anything.'

They had been sitting there in peace and silence for a few minutes, two of them writing, one reading, the fourth looking out of the window and the fifth dozing, when Natascha noticed something very peculiar about her book.

One of the pages was upside down.

If she hadn't read the book before, she might have suspected that the page was supposed to be printed upside down. She might have believed that the author was having a joke, for instance, or making sure her readers hadn't dozed off. However, Natascha had read *Harry Potter and the Deathly Hallows* once already and she was almost sure that, the first time, all the pages had been printed the right way up.

Some people complain about the smallest things. Not Natascha. If her feet got wet or her dinner was cold or the train was late, she just kept walking or eating or waiting. She didn't like making a fuss. She preferred to deal with problems herself without bothering anyone else. Now, she simply turned the book upside down and read the page, then turned the book the right way up again and continued reading.

Or, at least, she tried to continue reading. But the next page was upside down too. And the one after that. And the following two.

This was getting weird.

Rather than read any further, Natascha flicked through the book, searching for more upside-down pages. She found at least twenty. Even worse, she discovered that the text jumped straight from page 262 to 314. All the pages in between were missing.

Although Natascha had already read the book and

knew what happened, she wasn't very pleased to discover that she'd bought a copy with twenty pages printed upside down and fifty more missing.

She showed the book to the others and explained what she'd found.

'I don't understand,' said Mrs Malt. 'What on earth has happened? I've never seen a book like this before.'

'I'll tell you exactly what's happened,' said Mr Malt. 'Natascha has been sold a pirate copy. That's what comes of buying books from boys on trains. Much better to buy a book in a bookshop.'

'I don't understand,' said Natascha. 'Do you mean this book has been made by pirates?'

'That's exactly what I mean,' said Mr Malt. 'I read an article about Indian pirates in the *Financial Times*. Apparently, it's a terrible problem.'

That sounds interesting, thought Tim. He liked the thought of pirates. Maybe, if they'd printed this book, they might still be roaming through the train and he would get to meet them. He said, 'What kind of pirates?'

Mr Malt explained that these pirates didn't have eye patches, hooks for hands or parrots on their shoulders. Instead, they just had big factories where they printed fake books, CDs and DVDs. 'That's why it was so cheap,' said Mr Malt. 'The pirates buy one copy of the book, scan the pages into a computer and print hundreds more. They use cheap paper and poor-quality ink too. Look – it's all over your fingers.'

Mr Malt was right. Natascha's fingers were covered in

black ink, which had smudged from the pages of her book. Dirty streaks ran down her thumbs, across her palms and even onto her clothes.

Tim lifted his camera and took several shots of Natascha's blackened fingers and the book, making sure that he captured the upside-down pages. If the police ever caught the pirates, he wanted to have evidence of what they'd done.

Mrs Malt fished a tissue from her bag and passed it to Natascha, who carefully wiped her hands.

Tim had been disappointed to learn that he wasn't going to meet any pirates – even Indian pirates without eye patches, hooks for hands or parrots on their shoulders – but he hadn't forgotten Krishnan. He stood up and whistled to Grk. 'Come on! Let's go!'

Grk jumped to his feet and started barking excitedly.

'Come on, Natascha!' Tim beckoned. 'You should come too.'

Natascha said, 'Where?'

'To get your money back,' said Tim. 'He can't have gone anywhere. The train hasn't stopped. If we walk through the carriages from one end of the train to the other, we'll find him.'

As Natascha started to stand up, Mrs Malt said, 'Sit down. And you too, Tim.'

Tim said, 'Why?'

'Just come and sit here beside me, please.'

'But why?'

'Because you're not going anywhere.'

'Why not?'

'Because you can't just wander up and down an Indian train.'

'Why not?'

'Because anything might happen.'

'Like what?'

'You could get mugged, for instance. Or kidnapped. You wouldn't want that to happen, would you?'

'But Mum—'

'No buts,' said Mrs Malt. 'You're not going anywhere and that's final. I'm sorry, Natascha, but it's really not the end of the world.' She leaned across the compartment and took the book from Natascha. 'Look, it's only a book, and a very cheap book too. You can buy another one when we get home. Can't you?'

Natascha shrugged her shoulders. 'I guess so.'

Tim said, 'But Mum—'

'Didn't you hear what I said? No buts. Now, sit down and stop making such a fuss. We'll be there soon.' Mrs Malt put the damaged book on the seat beside her. 'Natascha, you've got lots of other books to read. Why don't you read one of them?'

'Sure,' said Natascha. She picked up her copy of Mahatma Gandhi's autobiography and tried to find her place.

Speaking quickly so his mother wouldn't have time to interrupt, Tim said, 'We wouldn't get mugged or kidnapped. We'd just go down the train and find that boy and give him the book and get our money and come straight back here, I promise.'

'Tim,' said Mrs Malt.

'Yes, Mum?'

'That's enough.'

Somehow, Mrs Malt said those two words in such a way that Tim knew there was absolutely no point arguing. He sighed, slumped into his seat and stared out of the window.

Grk looked at Tim for a moment, wondering what was going on. Were they going for a walk or weren't they? Reluctantly, Grk was forced to conclude that they weren't. He walked three times in a circle, lay down on the floor, closed his eyes and went back to sleep.

Chapter 7

All around Agra Station there were a hundred loudspeakers. A voice boomed announcements from the control room, explaining which trains were leaving from which platforms and when. The voice spoke first in Hindi, then in English. 'The express from New Delhi to Agra Cantonment, due at ten thirty-five, has now arrived on platform three. This train has been delayed by one hour and twenty minutes. The inconvenience caused is deeply regretted.'

The train pulled slowly into the station. Doors swung open. Impatient passengers flung themselves onto the platform before the train had even stopped and jogged towards the exit.

The brakes squealed. The wheels turned slower and slower. With a final judder, the train eased to a standstill.

Inside coach A1, two children peered out of the window, worried and excited by what they could see.

They watched hundreds of people pouring out of the doors, surging onto the platform. They listened to the shouts and screams that filled the air. They stared at the porters in red uniforms who ran alongside the train, yelling in several languages, offering to help with bags and cases.

There was so much to see and hear, they might have been happy to sit there all day, but a loud voice interrupted them with these words: 'Come on, kids! This is where we get off. We're late already. An hour and twenty minutes – it's ridiculous. Fetch your luggage. Put the lead on the dog. Come on, come on! Let's get going!'

Mr Malt had already gathered his coat, his hat, his newspaper and his bag. His wife was ready too. Now, the pair of them waited impatiently while the two children turned away from the window and grabbed their possessions. Natascha stuffed her books in her rucksack. Tim kneeled on the floor and attached the lead to Grk's collar. He looked around to check that they hadn't left anything behind. On the seat, he saw a book. He said, 'Natascha, you've left your book behind.'

'I don't want it,' said Natascha.

'But you paid three hundred rupees for it.'

'That's only four pounds. Anyway, what use is a book with fifty pages missing?'

Mr Malt was getting increasingly impatient. He said, 'Everyone ready? Can we go yet? Or do you want to spend the whole day standing here chatting?'

'We're ready and waiting,' said Mrs Malt. 'Aren't we?'

The two children nodded. Grk wagged his tail.

'Then let's go,' said Mr Malt. 'Whatever you do, don't get lost! We're late enough already. I don't want to waste what remains of the day searching for you. Come on! Let's go! Follow me!'

He led the way down the carriage towards the door. Mrs Malt hurried after him, followed by Natascha.

Before joining the others, Tim grabbed the discarded book. It seemed stupid to abandon a brand new book just because fifty pages were missing. He tucked it under his arm and hurried after the others.

A great mass of people were crammed around the door, some waiting to get off and others waiting to get on, crushed together so tightly that no one seemed able to move. After a lot of pushing and shoving, Mr Malt managed to force his way out of the door, then stepped down onto the platform. 'Come on,' he shouted to the rest of his family. 'This way! Don't lose sight of one another! Follow me!'

Mrs Malt pushed through the crowd and managed to rejoin her husband. Tim, Grk and Natascha followed close behind. The five of them forced their way down the platform, squeezed through a doorway and emerged in the main hall of Agra Railway Station.

Immediately, they were surrounded by a crowd of taxi drivers and guides, all pushing forward, all shouting, all promising that they were the cheapest and the best. Their voices blended into a blur of words: 'Here! Mister! Mister! You want guide! You want driver! Taj Mahal! One hundred rupees, very good price! Fixed price. Government price. Fifty rupees only! Mister, mister! Here! Mister! Mister! You want hotel? Good hotel? Best price! Best price!'

Mr Malt had no patience with them. 'We're not interested, thank you very much,' he said briskly, pushing past the touts. 'We have a taxi already. We're being met by a driver, thank you. Can't you just leave us alone?'

Gradually, the guides and taxi drivers realised that Mr Malt wasn't going to be persuaded. They drifted away and started searching for other tourists who had come to Agra on the same train.

When the family was finally alone, Mrs Malt turned to her husband and said, 'We're being met by a car, are we?'

'Yes, dear,' said Mr Malt. 'I arranged it yesterday. A taxi will be waiting at the station to drive us directly to the Taj Mahal.'

'And where exactly is this car?'

'I told you already, dearest. The driver will be waiting for us when we leave the train.'

'And just where will he be waiting for us?'

'Right here in the station.'

'And how will we know who he is?'

'He'll be holding a sign with our name on.'

Mrs Malt turned her head slowly from side to side, looking around the station, then reverted her attention to her husband. 'I'm probably being terribly stupid, dearest. But I can't see anyone in this station holding a sign with our name on. Can you?'

After Mr Malt had looked all around the station, he was forced to admit that he couldn't. He pulled out his mobile phone and called the travel agent in Delhi who had arranged their trip.

Because the train had been an hour late, the travel agent explained over the phone, the taxi had taken another passenger to the Taj Mahal instead. Before Mr Malt had a chance to say how annoying this was, the travel agent promised to send another taxi as quickly as possible and, cutting off Mr Malt just as he was starting to protest, put the phone down.

'The driver won't be here for another twenty minutes,' sighed Mr Malt. 'Well, he said twenty minutes, but I wouldn't be surprised if he took an hour and twenty minutes.' He shook his head. 'This country... I just can't believe it. Everything takes so long!'

They put their luggage in a pile and settled down to wait. Grk walked three times in a circle, lay down on the ground, closed his eyes and went to sleep. Mr Malt read his newspaper. Mrs Malt and Natascha read their books. Tim didn't feel like reading, so he just stared at the crowds that surrounded them, watching people hurrying to and from the platforms, wondering where they were all going.

A billion people live in India.

There are seven billion people living on the entire planet. So, one in every seven human beings is an Indian citizen.

That's why India is such a crowded country.

Of course, there are some places in India which aren't crowded. If you go to the mountains or the deserts, for instance, you won't see many people. But if you go to the cities, you'll see more people than you've ever seen in your entire life.

Tim didn't mind. He liked watching all the people, seeing how India looked different from home. Even better, he liked taking photos. He lifted his camera and surreptitiously snapped shots of anyone or anything that looked interesting.

Suddenly, Grk opened his eyes. His nostrils twitched. His ears wriggled. He growled very softly.

Tim was the only person who noticed. He glanced at Grk, then looked across the crowded foyer, following the direction of Grk's eyes, but he couldn't see anything worth growling at. He could just see a huge crowd of men and women of all ages, shapes and sizes, pouring in and out of the doors that led to the platforms.

Grk growled again, a little louder.

He must have seen another dog, thought Tim. Or perhaps a cat. He wrapped the lead around his wrist, keeping a tight grip, making sure that Grk couldn't escape.

Grk growled once more, even louder.

Tim was just about to scold him when – Yes! There! – he saw exactly what Grk was growling at.

On the other side of the foyer, just visible through the crowds, Tim could see a skinny boy wearing dark trousers, a beige shirt and sandals. In his right hand, the boy was carrying a big plastic bag. He was walking towards the exit. In a moment, he would have left the station. And then he would be gone forever.

It was Krishnan.

Tim knew exactly what he had to do.

Moving very slowly and casually, trying to show no sign of the excitement that he was feeling, Tim pulled himself to his feet. Keeping the pirated book tucked under his arm, he gave Grk's lead a quick tug.

Grk knew immediately what was happening. He sprang to his feet, his tail wagging, his tongue drooping from his jaws, and strained at the lead, impatient to explore his surroundings.

'I'm going to take Grk for a quick walk,' said Tim. 'I think he needs a pee.'

Mrs Malt looked at her son for a moment, trying to decide whether to trust him. She said, 'Can't he wait?'

'He has been on a train for hours. He's allowed a pee, isn't he?'

'You won't go far, will you?'

'No, Mum.'

'Do you promise?'

'Yes, Mum. I promise.'

'Where exactly are you going to go?'

'Just out there.' Tim pointed at the exit. 'He'll have a pee and then we'll come straight back again.'

'Go on, then,' said Mrs Malt. 'But don't—'

We'll never know what Mrs Malt was going to say next, or what she didn't want Tim to do, because Tim and Grk were already hurrying across the platform, darting through the crowd, heading in the direction that Krishnan had taken.

Chapter 8

Tim had a simple plan. It should only take a couple of minutes. Maybe three. Or five at the most. He would grab Krishnan and demand a full refund of three hundred rupees for the pirated book. Armed with the cash, he'd hurry back to his parents, who would hardly have noticed his absence. There should even be time for Grk to have a pee. Everyone would be happy – especially Natascha, when he presented her with the three hundred rupees.

Almost immediately, the plan started going wrong.

Have you ever tried to move quickly across a big crowded room?

If you have, you'll know that it's not easy. Whichever way you go, someone seems to be standing in your path. Legs and luggage block every route. Speed is impossible.

Tim and Grk ducked round passengers and squeezed through queues, apologising whenever they bumped into someone. By the time they finally emerged at the station's main entrance, two minutes had probably passed already.

Lorries, cars and bicycles rushed up and down the busy road. Horns hooted. Engines roared. People yelled and screamed. Tim felt as if he was standing on the edge of an ocean made of noise and colour and movement rather than water. If he stepped off the pavement and into the road, he would be swept away.

There was no sign of Krishnan. He must have crossed this road and gone into the city. In this chaos, there was no hope of finding him.

Tim sighed. He looked at Grk. 'As we've come out here, you might as well have a pee.'

Grk took no notice. He didn't even show any sign that he wanted to pee. His ears were raised, his tail was wagging slowly from side to side and he was pulling on his lead.

Tim peered in the direction that Grk wanted to go.

He could see a boy. A slim, dark boy in tatty clothing.

But it wasn't the boy from the train.

'That's not him,' said Tim. 'That's not Krishnan.'

Grk took no notice. He pulled harder at the lead. He was desperate to follow the boy.

'Thanks very much for trying to help,' said Tim. 'But I've got to tell you, Grk, you've got the wrong boy. That's not Krishnan. That's someone completely different.'

Grk glanced at Tim for a moment, then returned all his attention to the boy, tugging even harder on the lead.

In a couple of seconds, the boy would have disappeared. If Tim and Grk were going to follow him, they'd have to do it now.

Tim didn't know what to do. Should he trust Grk?

Perhaps the boy worked in a butcher's shop.

Perhaps he was carrying a delicious-smelling bag of bones. Or Grk might just have got completely confused and thought the boy was Krishnan.

But Grk wasn't the sort of dog who got confused. Grk was right about most things.

In many ways, Tim trusted Grk more than he trusted himself.

'Okay,' said Tim. 'Let's follow that boy.'

Together, Tim and Grk sprinted down the street and followed the boy back into the railway station.

As the boy pushed through the crowds, he never once glanced over his shoulder. He obviously didn't have any reason to suspect that he was being followed.

Behind him, Tim and Grk hopped over outstretched legs and dodged round suitcases, trying to keep the boy within sight at all times. They followed him up a flight of stairs and over the walkway which crossed the tracks. Above them, big notice boards displayed the number of each platform, the time that the next train would leave and where it was going.

When the boy reached platforms twelve and thirteen, he turned to the left and headed down another flight of stairs.

Tim and Grk hurried to catch up. At the bottom of the stairs, they found themselves on a packed platform, jammed with people waiting for the next train to arrive. There was no sign of the boy.

If Tim had been alone, he wouldn't have had a clue what to do and most probably would have stood there for a few minutes, feeling hopeless, before turning round and walking back to his parents. Luckily, he was with Grk, who seemed to know exactly what to do and which way to go. Being a dog and therefore possessing very sensitive nostrils, Grk might have been able to smell the boy. Or perhaps, being so much shorter than Tim and therefore closer on the ground, he could see things that Tim couldn't. For whatever reason, Grk trotted down the platform without a moment's hesitation and wove through the crowd, pulling Tim on the lead behind him.

When they had been walking for a couple of minutes, the crowds thinned, and Tim saw the boy again.

He had reached the end of the platform and was just about to jump off.

Don't jump, thought Tim. You'll electrocute yourself.

Without a moment's hesitation, the boy leaped off the platform and down onto the tracks. He gave a quick glance to left and right to check that no trains were coming, and then walked across the rails.

Tim and Grk hurried along the platform until they reached the place where the boy had jumped down onto the tracks. They stood on the edge of the platform, looking left, then right, then left again.

Tim had never walked across railway tracks. At home, if you had to cross from one platform to another, you used a tunnel or a bridge. You didn't just hop off the platform and stroll across the tracks.

If the tracks were electrified, he would be fried.

If a train came, he would be squished, squashed, splatted and chopped into a hundred pieces.

But what else could he do? There was no other way to cross the tracks.

Tim jumped. And Grk jumped with him.

Chapter 9

Tim and Grk landed in the gravel beside the rails. They didn't get electrocuted or run over. They just hopped over the rails and hurried after the boy, trying to keep him in sight.

On this side of the railway tracks, there was a metal fence, marking the boundary of the railway station, and a series of sidings, filled with engines and carriages. Passengers weren't allowed here. This was where the railway's employees cleaned and repaired the trains when they weren't being used.

There was rubbish everywhere. Paper and plastic bags fluttered in the breeze. The whole place stank like a toilet. There was a simple reason for that: it had been used as a toilet. Piles of poo had been scattered on the gravel. They might have been left by dogs, pigs or even people. Tim trod carefully, watching where he put his feet, not wanting to step in something unpleasant.

Tim and Grk had been walking for a few moments, ducking round stationary carriages and walking over more tracks, when they saw fifteen or twenty boys clustered in a group. Tim recognised a slim boy holding a plastic bag. It was Krishnan! Grk had been right. The boy had led them exactly where they wanted to go.

'You're a genius,' whispered Tim.

Grk wagged his tail faster as if to say: 'Have you only just noticed?'

Together, Tim and Grk hurried towards the group of boys. As they came closer, Tim counted them. There were nineteen. He started to feel a bit nervous. There was one of him against nineteen of them. Yes, of course, he had Grk on his side, but that didn't make much difference. One boy and a dog against nineteen boys – it was impossible! What could he do against so many? If they decided to push him around or steal his money, he wouldn't be able to put up any resistance. His screams wouldn't be heard by anyone. They could do whatever they wanted to him and no one would know.

Tim considered turning round and hurrying away before the nineteen boys noticed him. He could go back to his parents and ask for their help. Or find a policeman in the station.

No. That was hopeless. By the time he came back with his parents or the police, the boys would have gone. If he was going to get some compensation for the damaged book, he had to do it now. And he had to do it himself. He walked across the gravel, tapped one of the boys on the shoulder and said, 'Hello, Krishnan.'

Nineteen heads turned to see who had spoken. Thirty-eight eyes stared at Tim and Grk.

All the boys looked much the same. They were dirty and dishevelled. Their clothes were covered with holes. Only a few had shoes and the rest were barefoot. Most were carrying plastic bags, just like Krishnan's, and several were holding plastic water bottles. Piled against a brick wall, there were at least a hundred more empty plastic water bottles, the tops tied together with string.

When the nineteen boys saw Tim, some looked surprised and others looked nervous, but one just grinned.

'Hello, Mister Tim,' said Krishnan.

'Hi,' said Tim.

If Krishnan was feeling worried or guilty, he didn't show it. He turned to the other boys in the group. 'This is Mister Tim. He is one fine Englishman. He is excellent at cricket. Mister Tim is a personal friend of both Mister Ian Botham and Mister Andrew Flintoff.'

The boys started chattering amongst themselves, impressed by this unexpected piece of information. Tim tried to explain that he didn't actually know Andrew Flintoff or Ian Botham, and didn't even much like cricket, but no one seemed to take any notice of his explanations.

In a loud voice, speaking over the top of everyone else, Krishnan said, 'So, Mister Tim, do you want to play one game of cricket? England versus India? Yes?'

'No, thanks,' said Tim. 'I'd rather talk about Harry Potter.' He pulled out the copy of *Harry Potter and the Deathly Hallows*.

'Oh, yes. Harry Potter! A very good book. A very English book. Now, Mister Tim, you must tell me the absolute truth. Do you like your new book?'

'No,' said Tim. 'I don't like it at all.'

'No? Why not?'

'Because it's missing some of its pages. And others are upside down. This isn't a proper book. You sold us a bad copy.'

Krishnan said, 'You want one replacement?'

Tim was surprised. He hadn't expected the negotiations to be so straightforward. He nodded. 'Yes, please.'

'No problem.' Krishnan knelt on the ground and opened his plastic bag. He selected a new copy of *Harry Potter and the Deathly Hallows* and handed it to Tim, taking the damaged copy in exchange.

Tim took the book and thanked him.

'No problem,' said Krishnan. 'You happy, me happy. Am I right, Mister Tim?'

'You're right,' said Tim. 'You're happy and I'm happy. Everyone's happy.'

Eager to show off what he had achieved, Tim was just about to hurry back to Natascha and his parents, carrying the new book, when something occurred to him. What if there was a problem with this book too? He turned over the front cover and ran through the pages.

Almost immediately, he found a page that was printed upside down. Flicking further through the book, he found another upside-down page, and then another, and then several more, until he realised that there must have been at least twenty pages printed upside down.

When he searched further into the book, he saw that, just like the other copy, pages 262 to 314 were completely missing.

'This is no good,' said Tim, thrusting the book back at Krishnan and flicking quickly through the pages to show him that some were upside down and others missing. 'You've given me another damaged copy. I want a book with all its pages.'

'No problem,' said Krishnan. 'I give you one replacement.' He took the book from Tim's hands, stuffed it back inside his plastic bag and pulled out yet another copy of the same book.

This time, Tim wasn't taking any risks. He took the book and flicked through the pages.

It was exactly as he had suspected. Just like the others, this copy had twenty upside-down pages and at least fifty missing. All the copies shared the same faults. Handing the book back, Tim said, 'That's no good either. I don't want a damaged book, I want a refund.'

'No problem,' said Krishnan. 'You want one new book? One not Harry Potter book?' Before Tim could answer, Krishnan reached into another boy's bag and pulled out a different book. 'How about this one? No? Well, how about some music?' He grabbed a bunch of CDs from another boy's bag. 'You like music?'

'I just want my money back,' said Tim.

'How about a movie? You like movies?'

'Of course I like movies,' said Tim. 'But I'd rather have my money back.'

'Here you go, have a movie. Much better than money. Do you prefer Hollywood or Bollywood?' Krishnan reached into another boy's bag and pulled out several DVDs. Some were recent American movies and others were Indian movies that Tim had never even heard of.

'Here, we have all sorts. Hollywood and Bollywood. Pick one, Mister Tim. Any one. What would you like?'

Tim realised that each of the boys was carrying a selection of different books, CDs and DVDs in their bags. All of them seemed to be brand new. Some actually looked quite interesting, but Tim refused to be tempted. Just as he was now sure that all of Krishnan's books had missing pages and ink that smudged, he didn't trust Krishnan's CDs or DVDs either. When the CDs were played they'd probably get stuck. And the films would probably have fuzzy pictures or scenes missing so the plot made no sense.

'I don't want another book or a movie or any music,' said Tim. 'I've had enough of your stuff. I just want my money back.'

'No problem,' said Krishnan. He stood up, holding a copy of *Harry Potter and the Deathly Hallows*. It might even have been the one which Natascha originally bought. 'Here. You take this. Go on, take this. It is one good book.'

'That's not a good book,' said Tim. 'In fact, it's not even a book, it's only part of a book. It's missing fifty pages. Look, how many times do I have to say this? I don't want one of your books, I want my money back.'

'Sorry, this is not possible.'

'Why not?'

'Because I have no money,' said Krishnan with a sad smile. He pulled out the lining of his pockets, showing they were empty. 'All my money is gone.'

'Gone?'

'Yes. Precisely. All gone.'

'Where can it have gone? You've only just got off the train. You haven't had time to spend any money.'

'No, the money is not spent.'

'Then where is it?'

'I have given it all to Gunyan.'

'Gunyan? What are you talking about? Who's Gunyan?'

'I am Gunyan,' said a deep voice.

Tim and Grk both turned round to see where the voice was coming from.

They found themselves facing a tall, broad-shouldered man with dark eyes and a cruel mouth. In his left ear, the man had a small silver ring. He was wearing blue jeans and a white shirt with baggy sleeves. Perhaps he had just arrived or perhaps he had been standing there for some time, listening to the conversation.

'I am Gunyan,' repeated the man, his voice even deeper and more menacing than before. 'My question is – who are you?'

Chapter 10

Tim stared at Gunyan, trying not to show the slightest sign of the fear that he was feeling. 'My name is Tim,' he said. 'And this is Grk.' He pointed at Grk.

Whenever Grk heard his name being spoken, he usually wagged his tail. But not this time. Instead, he just fixed his eyes on Gunyan, carefully watching every move that the man made.

'Tim and Grk,' repeated Gunyan, looking from the boy to the dog and back again, nodding slowly. 'And you are from which country?'

'England,' said Tim.

'Ah, England.' Gunyan's lips lifted in a wide smile, which was strange, because no one had said or done anything particularly amusing. 'And tell me now, Tim, what are you and your friend Grk doing in Agra? Have you come here to see the Taj Mahal?'

'Yes.'

'Very good, very good.' Gunyan's smile seemed to get even broader. He lifted his right arm and gripped Krishnan around the neck. 'You know this boy? He is also one of your friends?'

'No, I don't know him,' said Tim. 'When I was coming here on the train from Delhi, he sold me this book.' Tim held up his copy of *Harry Potter and the Deathly Hallows*. 'But it's a damaged copy. Some pages are missing. And some have been printed upside down. So I came to get my money back.'

'Give me the book,' said Gunyan, holding out his right hand.

'Why?'

'Just give it to me.'

Tim didn't like being ordered around by someone whom he'd never met before. But Gunyan was a lot bigger and stronger than him. He knew there wasn't any point trying to resist. He placed the book in Gunyan's outstretched hand.

Gunyan grabbed the book.

Without pausing to glance inside, as if he knew what he was going to find there before he'd even looked, Gunyan turned on Krishnan and said, 'You have cheated a tourist! A visitor to our country! What are you thinking of?'

Rather than answering in English, Krishnan replied in Hindi, so Tim had no idea what he was saying.

If Krishnan thought that speaking in Hindi would make Gunyan behave more kindly towards him, he was wrong. Hardly giving Krishnan time to say more than a few words, Gunyan lifted the book with his right hand and, in a single sudden movement, which was as shocking for its speed as its violence, brought the heavy book crashing down on the top of Krishnan's head.

With a cry of agony, Krishnan staggered backwards, clutching his skull.

'This will show you!' shouted Gunyan, speaking English now. Raising the book above his head once again, he advanced on the boy. 'Never cheat an honest tourist! Never cheat a visitor to our country! You will give all of India a very bad name! Do you understand what I am saying? Do you?'

Without waiting for an answer, Gunyan brought the book crashing down on Krishnan's head again. This blow was so strong that Krishnan collapsed in a heap on the ground, holding his head with both hands and moaning piteously.

Tim watched what was happening with horror. He wanted to stop the big man hurting the small boy. And yet he hardly dared even say anything, because he was scared he might get beaten too. He was a small boy in a foreign country. What could he do to stop a grown man attacking another small boy?

He glanced at the circle of eighteen other boys who were watching the fight, wondering why none of them made any move to intervene. They just stood there, their arms hanging uselessly by their sides, watching a man beat their friend to the ground. If they had all joined together, they could have stopped Gunyan. But none of them moved.

It looked as if the beating was going to get even worse. Krishnan was crouching on the floor, clutching his head and weeping in agony, but Gunyan didn't take pity on him. The big man drew his arm back, lifting the book into the air, preparing to deliver one more blow.

Not thinking, hardly even knowing what he was doing, Tim jumped forward and grabbed the book with both hands. 'Stop!' he shouted. 'Stop hitting him!'

*

At that moment, before anyone had time to move or speak, Tim saw something very surprising.

He was staring at the back of Gunyan's head. He wouldn't have noticed it otherwise. But with all his attention fixed on Gunyan's skull, he noticed a small blue blotch behind Gunyan's right ear.

Usually, the tattoo would have remained hidden. And even if it had been exposed, the tattoo was so small and so dark that most people wouldn't have paid it much attention. Almost anyone else would have mistaken it for a birthmark or a wart or a bit of dirt which had got stuck to Gunyan's skin.

But Tim had sharp eyesight and he could see that the blue blotch was a tattoo. He could also see exactly what it represented.

A small blue rat with a long wriggly tail.

Before Tim had had time to remember where and when he had seen exactly the same tattoo before, Gunyan whirled round, his left hand raised, his fist clenched and ready to punch. But, before he could smack his fist into the side of Tim's face, a growl filled the air.

A low, angry growl.

It came from the ground near Tim's feet.

Gunyan, Krishnan and the eighteen other boys turned to look at the source of the noise.

They saw a small dog with beady black eyes, white fur with black patches and a perky little tail.

Grk's mouth was open. His teeth were bared. His eyes were fixed on Gunyan.

Although Grk couldn't speak, the meaning of his growl was completely clear: 'If you don't drop your fist,' he was saying, 'I'll bite you.'

'And I should probably warn you,' Grk's growl added, 'my teeth may be small but they are extremely sharp.'

Chapter 11

Gunyan was the first to move. He took a step backwards and smiled at Tim.

'I like you,' he said. 'You are a good boy. There is no need for us to fight. We can be friends, not enemies.'

Tim would have liked to say 'I don't like you' and 'I don't want to be your friend' but he didn't. It's never a good idea to insult people who are twice your size. Instead, he said, 'You shouldn't have hit Krishnan.'

'Why not?'

'Because you hurt him. Look!' Tim pointed at Krishnan, who was still squatting on the floor, rubbing his bruised skull with one hand and wiping away his tears with the other.

Gunyan glanced at Krishnan and his smile seemed to grow even wider. 'That is right, I have hurt him. But I have hurt him because it is right to hurt him.'

'What do you mean? How can it be right to hurt someone?'

'If a boy does a bad thing, as this boy has, then he must be punished. He sold you a bad book. So he must be punished.'

'I don't care about the book,' said Tim. 'Just don't hurt him any more. Leave him alone, please.'

'You are a very kind boy,' said Gunyan. 'But this is

not your country. You do not understand how things work here.'

'I understand one thing,' said Tim. 'You shouldn't hit someone half your size.'

'Even if he is a thief? This boy is a dirty little thief and thieves must be punished! Maybe not in your country. Maybe in England, a thief will be allowed to go free and continue thieving all night and all day. But in my country, we punish thieves. Otherwise, everybody will become a thief and nothing will be safe.'

Tim wanted to argue, but Gunyan didn't give him a chance.

'Go now,' said Gunyan, making a dismissive gesture with his right hand, as if he was brushing crumbs from a table. 'There's nothing here for you. You can't have your three hundred rupees back again because this little thief has already spent them. So, you should just go. Go and see the Taj Mahal like a good tourist.'

Tim pointed at Krishnan. 'What will happen to him?'

'That is his business,' said Gunyan. 'And mine also. But not yours. Go on, go now. Go!'

Tim glanced at Krishnan.

For a moment, their eyes met. A look passed between them. Neither of them would have been able to describe what that look meant, but both of them would have agreed that it meant something important.

Gunyan was getting impatient. 'Go now,' he said. 'You don't have any business with us. Go!' He walked towards Tim, clenching his fists.

Grk growled once more, but Gunyan didn't care. He

was a big man with strong arms. He wouldn't have any trouble beating a boy and a small dog – even a dog as fierce and courageous as Grk.

There are some fights you can win. And some you can't.

Maybe Grk didn't know that, but Tim did.

Without saying another word, Tim turned his back on Gunyan, Krishnan and the eighteen other boys, and walked briskly away, tugging Grk alongside him.

Together, the boy and the dog turned the corner, crossed the railway tracks and clambered back onto platform thirteen.

Chapter 12

Mrs Malt realised she had made a terrible mistake. She shouldn't have let Tim take Grk for a walk. He wasn't old enough to explore an Indian railway station alone.

As the minutes passed, and there was still no sign of her son, she began to fear the worst. What if he'd been robbed? Or kidnapped? What if he'd been run over by a car or fallen in front of a train? What if he was wandering around another part of the station, lost and lonely, trying to find his way back again?

'We've got to do something,' said Mrs Malt. 'We can't just stand here. Let's go and look for him.'

'We can't all go wandering off,' replied Mr Malt. 'Tim might come back here. He won't know where we've gone. We should stay exactly where we are and wait for him to come back.'

'I'll stay here,' said Mrs Malt. 'You can go and look for him.'

'Me? What if I get lost too?'

'It won't be the end of the world,' said Mrs Malt. 'Go on, Terence. Go and find him.'

Natascha sat on the ground, trying to ignore the Malts' voices and concentrate on reading her book. She wasn't worried about Tim. She knew he could look after himself. And if he couldn't, Grk would look after him instead. Sooner or later, the two of them would come back again.

'Fine, I'll look for him,' said Mr Malt. 'But please, Melanie, don't go anywhere. Just stay here and wait for me to come back.'

'Don't come back without Tim,' said Mrs Malt.

'No, dear. I wouldn't dream of it.' With a resigned expression on his face, Mr Malt started walking away from his wife. He had taken about ten paces when he ran straight into a small boy and a dog.

'Hi, Dad,' said Tim.

Mr Malt stared at his son. He was so surprised, he couldn't think of anything to say. And before he could, Mrs Malt had joined them.

'Hi, Mum,' said Tim.

Mrs Malt's voice was shaking. She was so upset that she could hardly speak. She said, 'Where on earth have you been?'

'I took Grk for a pee. Just like I said I would.'

'But you've been gone for hours!'

'He had a long pee.'

'This isn't the time for jokes,' said Mrs Malt. 'Your father and I have been extremely worried. We didn't know what had happened to you! You can't just wander off, Tim. Not in a place like this. Do you understand why not?'

'Yes, Mum,' said Tim. 'I might get mugged or murdered.'

'We can discuss all this later,' said Mr Malt, tapping the face of his watch. 'We've wasted enough time already. At this rate, we won't even have time to see the Taj Mahal before we have to get the train back to Delhi.'

Walking on either side of Tim like two prison warders guarding a dangerous prisoner, Mr and Mrs Malt led their son through the railway station and out into the street. Natascha followed a few paces behind, holding Grk's lead.

As they walked, Mrs Malt had a few stern words with Tim, telling him never to run away again. She explained that India was a dangerous country and no one should wander round on their own. She said, 'Do you promise that you will never do that again?'

'I promise,' said Tim.

Outside the station, the taxi was waiting. They clambered inside. The driver and the guide sat in the front. Mr Malt, Mrs Malt, Tim, Natascha and Grk crammed into the back.

The guide turned around and introduced himself. 'Good morning, hello, welcome to Agra. My name is Ram. I will be your guide today. Are you ready to see the most beautiful building in the world?'

'Oh, yes,' said Mr Malt. 'We're more than ready. In fact, we've been ready for the past hour. We've just been waiting for you to turn up.'

'Very good,' said the guide with a big grin. 'Then let us go and see the Taj Mahal!' He turned round and tapped the driver's shoulder. With a lurch, the car accelerated away from the railway station and joined the traffic heading towards the centre of the city.

Chapter 13

At the entrance to the Taj Mahal, beggars sat in the dust, stretching out their hands. Children ran up and down the street, asking for coins. Salesmen offered T-shirts, books, pamphlets, postcards and little white models of the Taj Mahal. Dogs, pigs, chickens and cows wandered freely through the crowds, nuzzling the road, searching for scraps.

A group of uniformed soldiers divided visitors into two queues, one for men and one for women, then directed them through a metal detector, preventing anyone from bringing guns, knives or other weapons inside. In the queue for men, the soldiers let Mr Malt through the metal detector, but stopped Tim. 'You stay here,' said one of the soldiers. 'You cannot go any further.'

'Why not?' said Tim.

'You are not permitted inside.'

'I don't have a gun,' said Tim. 'Or a knife. Or anything else made of metal.'

'But you have a dog,' said the soldier, pointing the barrel of his rifle at Grk. 'And no dogs are permitted inside the Taj Mahal.'

'Why not?'

The soldier pointed at a long notice pinned to the wall and printed with several hundred rules and regulations, explaining exactly what people could and couldn't do inside this important historical and archaeological site. 'As you will see if you read the rules and regulations, Rule 103B specifically permits no dogs inside the Taj Mahal. You can happily come inside, but the dog stays outside.'

'He can't stay outside on his own,' said Tim. 'He needs someone to look after him.'

The soldier shrugged his shoulders, not even bothering to pretend that he cared, and beckoned to the next people in the queue, inviting them to come forward.

After a brief discussion, the Malts decided that they would divide into two parties. First, Mrs Malt and Natascha would go inside with the guide and see the Taj Mahal. When they came out, Mr Malt and Tim would take a turn. Whoever stayed outside would look after Grk.

The guide led Natascha and Mrs Malt through the metal detector and took them into the Taj Mahal.

Mr Malt led Tim and Grk to a low brick wall opposite the entrance. They sat down. Mr Malt unfurled his newspaper and started reading. Grk walked three times in a circle and lay on the ground. Tim watched the soldiers and the tourists, listening to all the different languages that people were speaking.

Several people were walking up and down the lines of tourists, trying to sell them souvenirs or snacks. Tim wasn't interested in buying a T-shirt or any postcards, so he hadn't taken much notice of the salesmen, but he now noticed that one of them, a small boy with ragged clothes and no shoes, was holding a plastic bag packed with books.

Tim stood up and tugged Grk's lead. 'Come on,' he whispered. 'Let's see what he's selling.'

As Tim and Grk strolled towards the boy, Mr Malt called them back. 'Hey! Hey, Tim! Where do you think you're going?'

'I just want to see what that boy's selling.'

'Why?'

'I'd like another book.'

Mr Malt looked at his son for a moment, and then nodded. Books were educational. There couldn't be anything wrong with wanting another one. 'You won't go wandering off, will you?'

'No, Dad.'

'Go on, then. But be quick.'

Mr Malt returned to his newspaper. Tim and Grk strolled past the boy, lingering just long enough to see the book that he was offering to tourists. It was a copy of *Harry Potter and the Deathly Hallows*.

The boy noticed Tim's interest. 'Hello. Good morning. You want to buy one book?'

'I've already got it,' said Tim.

'You have this book? This Harry Potter?'

'Yes.'

'No problem. You want to buy one more book? What is your taste? You tell me what you like, I will find the perfect book for you.'

Tim said, 'Do you know a boy called Krishnan?'

'I know many boys called Krishnan,' said the boy. 'It is a very ordinary name in this country. Tell me more about this boy and perhaps I can help you.'

'He sold me a copy of that book,' said Tim, pointing at the boy's copy of *Harry Potter and the Deathly Hallows*. 'He was selling them on the train from Delhi and I bought one.'

'Sorry, sir, I do not know this boy.'

'How about a tall man with a silver earring? He said his name was Gunyan. Do you know him?'

When Tim said those words, something in the boy's expression changed and he stuffed his book back into the plastic bag. 'Very sorry, sir,' said the boy, not even lifting his head to meet Tim's eyes. 'I cannot help you.' He turned his back on Tim and walked briskly away.

Before the boy had taken more than a couple of paces, Tim did something which surprised even himself. He lunged forwards and grabbed the boy's right ear.

'Ow!' shrieked the boy.

Tim didn't let go.

'Owwwwww!' shrieked the boy even louder, wriggling desperately, trying to free himself from Tim's grip.

Tim still didn't let go.

In the queue, tourists turned to see what was happening. Some giggled. Others took photos.

Mr Malt didn't even lift his head from his newspaper. He was absorbed in a fascinating article about the computer industry in Bangalore.

Tim twisted the boy's ear so he could see what was tattooed to the other side. Yes! There it was! Exactly what he'd expected. On the underside of the boy's ear, there was a little tattoo of a blue rat with a long curly tail.

'What does this mean?' said Tim.

The boy didn't reply. He just stared at Tim, saying nothing.

'Tell me what's going on,' said Tim. 'Who are these people? Why are you scared of them?'

'I cannot tell you,' hissed the boy in a low whisper which couldn't be heard by anyone except Tim.

'Why not?'

'Because he kill me.'

'Who?'

'If he know me talk to you, he kill me. I no want to be dead.'

'Who will kill you?'

'The blue rat,' whispered the boy.

'The blue rat? What do you mean? Why are you so frightened of a *rat*?'

But the boy wasn't going to say another word. He yanked himself away from Tim, shaking himself free, and continued down the line of tourists. 'One book!' he shouted, displaying *Harry Potter and the Deathly Hallows* to the tourists in the queue. 'One book! One book! Who will buy one book?'

Chapter 14

Tim sat beside his father for half an hour, watching hundreds of tourists queuing to enter the Taj Mahal and hundreds more strolling out again. He could have read his book, but he didn't feel like reading. He would have preferred to go for a walk round the city, exploring the shops and cafés. Most of all, he would have liked to investigate the mystery of the blue rat tattoo. What did it mean? Where did it come from? What was the connection between all the different people who had the same tattoo in the same place on their ears?

Tim considered discussing these questions with his dad, then immediately dismissed the possibility. If you wanted to invest some money, buy a car or get a mortgage, Mr Malt was just the man to talk to. But if you wanted to solve a mystery of a blue rat tattoo, you'd be much better off asking someone else. If Tim had asked his father's advice and explained what he had discovered, Mr Malt would have been sure to say something like, 'Oh, it's just a coincidence. You happened to meet a few people who have the same taste in tattoos, that's all. As far as we know, half the men in India might have tattoos of little blue rats on the undersides of their ears. Now, why don't you read the guidebook and learn a few more useful facts about

Indian history? Don't you want to know who built the Taj Mahal?'

After half an hour, the guide emerged from the Taj Mahal with Natascha and Mrs Malt. They swapped over. Natascha took Grk from Tim and sat down to read her book. Mrs Malt sat beside her. Tim and Mr Malt went through the metal detectors and followed their guide into the Taj Mahal.

They walked across a courtyard, under a gateway and into the gardens that surrounded the Taj Mahal. Tim stared at the big white marble building. He listened to the guide's descriptions of who had built the Taj Mahal, and how, and why, and when. He took off his shoes and went inside. He looked at all the people taking photos and considered taking a few photos of his own, but decided not to bother.

When the three of them had walked all the way around the Taj Mahal, the guide turned to Mr Malt and Tim, and said, 'Now, you must tell me your thoughts and impressions. What is your honest opinion of the Taj Mahal? Or have you been made speechless by the splendour of the most beautiful building in the world?'

'It's certainly magnificent,' said Mr Malt.

'Indeed, sir, it is most magnificent.' With a big grin on his face, the guide turned to Tim. 'How about yourself, young man? Do you very much like the Taj Mahal? Have you ever seen another building to which it can be compared?'

'It's okay,' said Tim.

'Okay? Okay?' The guide laughed. 'Okay is all you can say?'

'Yes,' said Tim. 'It's okay.'

'That's all? Nothing more? You think the Taj Mahal does not deserve a better description than "okay"?'

'If you really want to know the truth,' said Tim, 'I think it's quite boring.'

The guide blinked a couple of times, then the smile slowly faded from his face. 'That is your opinion,' he said in a terse tone, as if he had taken Tim's words as a personal insult. 'And we are all entitled to our own opinion.' He turned his back on Tim and didn't address another word to him for the rest of the afternoon.

Chapter 15

At the entrance to the New Delhi Lawn Tennis Club, there was a wooden board with two words painted in big black letters.

NO DOGS

Not a single dog had ever been permitted to pass between the two tall iron gates of the New Delhi Lawn Tennis Club. The officials were worried that dogs would bark during the games, interrupting important points and distracting the players' attention. Even worse, they might pee on the grass.

Six guards in white uniforms stood at the gates, stopping anyone who didn't have a ticket and sending them away. And, of course, preventing a single dog from getting inside.

Tim and Grk were standing outside the New Delhi Lawn Tennis Club. They stared at the sign that said **NO DOGS** and listened to the sounds coming from the other side of the wall.

Tim wondered why the New Delhi Lawn Tennis Club was so prejudiced against dogs. What about cats? Why should they be allowed through the gates, but not dogs?

And what about camels? And giraffes? What about goats, grizzly bears and monkeys? If a zebra challenged an aardvark to a tennis match, would they be welcomed into the club?

What was so terrible about dogs?

The six guards in white uniforms looked extremely grumpy. Perhaps they hated their job. It certainly can't have been very interesting, standing there all day, checking tickets.

There wasn't much point quizzing them about the tennis club's anti-dog policy, thought Tim. They'd just tell him to stop asking such irritating questions.

Grk didn't bother reading the notice. Of course he didn't. Being a dog, he couldn't read. Instead, he sniffed the wooden post at the base of the sign, then lifted his leg and peed against it.

Just as Grk was finishing his pee, Mr Malt emerged from the New Delhi Lawn Tennis Club. He had been arguing with the officials who ran the club, trying to persuade them to let a dog inside. They had refused to change their minds.

'Rules are rules,' they had said. 'And the rules of the New Delhi Lawn Tennis Club state quite clearly that no dogs are allowed.'

Mr Malt looked at Tim and Grk. 'I'm sorry,' he said. 'We're going to have to spend the day in the hotel.'

Chapter 16

Inside the New Delhi Lawn Tennis Club, two young men were playing in the first match of the first round of the first Vijay Ghat International Lawn Tennis Association Under-Sixteen Championship.

Each of the young men was desperate to win. Each of them had been preparing for this match for weeks. Now, they were both ready to play the best tennis of their lives.

Their names were Troy Crown and Max Raffifi.

Troy Crown was fifteen years old. He was six foot three inches tall. He had broad shoulders and huge biceps. His blond, curly hair was tied into a ponytail with a piece of scarlet ribbon, given to him by one of his many female fans.

Troy had been born in Adelaide, a small city in Australia. At the age of two, he picked up a tennis racket for the first time. By the age of ten, he was competing in the Southern Australian Junior Championships. He won his first title on his twelfth birthday.

More than six hundred of Troy's fans had travelled to the New Delhi Lawn Tennis Club to cheer him on. Some lived in India. Others had flown all the way from Adelaide. They waved Australian flags and chanted his name. 'Troy! Troy! Troy! Troy is our boy! Troy! Troy! Troy! Troy is our boy!'

No one was shouting for Max. If he was going to win

this game, he'd have to do it alone. In fact, Max had only two supporters inside the tennis court and they were hardly even watching the match. As the shouts resounded around the court – 'Troy! Troy! Troy! Troy is our boy!' – neither of them took any notice. Mrs Malt was writing emails on her laptop, issuing instructions to her secretary's secretary. Natascha was hunched over her diary, scribbling a description of the Taj Mahal. Beside them there were two empty seats, where Tim and Mr Malt would have been sitting if they hadn't gone back to the hotel with Grk.

'Silence, please,' said the umpire. 'Troy Crown to serve.'

The crowd went quiet. Troy Crown bounced the ball twice on the ground, preparing to deliver the first serve of the match. He threw the ball into the air and whacked it with his racket.

The game had begun.

Troy Crown was famous for the speed of his serves. Today, he was on top form. The digital display in the corner of the court registered a speed of a hundred and two miles per hour. The ball swept past Max Raffifi, who couldn't even touch it with his racket.

'Fifteen-love,' said the umpire, but his voice could hardly be heard. The crowd had gone wild, shouting Troy's name and celebrating his success. He'd won the first point of the game. Now, they were sure, he'd go on to win all the others too.

Troy Crown grinned, turned to the ball boy, and clicked his fingers, demanding a new ball.

With that ball, he served another ace, winning the second point of the match. 'Thirty-love,' said the umpire. The crowd whooped and clapped and cheered.

Natascha just kept her head down and continued scribbling in her notebook.

Every day, she wrote a diary of everything that happened to her. She wrote about the weather. She wrote about the people that she had met, the food that she had eaten and the conversations that she had had. One day, she had decided, her journal would be published as a book.

There was a massive cheer from the crowd. 'Troy! Troy! Troy!'

Natascha paused in the middle of the sentence that she was writing, looked up from her notebook and saw Troy Crown punching the air with both his fists. He had won the third point. If he got the next point, he would have won the first game.

Natascha glanced across the court at her brother.

For a moment, their eyes met. Neither of them said a word. They didn't wink or wave or give any sign that they had even seen one another. But a kind of signal passed between them.

The umpire leaned forward, and spoke into his microphone. 'Forty-love. Quiet, please. Could we have silence, please.'

The crowd went quiet. People leaned forward in their seats. They watched and waited.

Troy Crown turned to one of the ball boys and clicked his fingers, demanding a new ball. The ball boy threw the ball to him.

Troy bounced the ball a couple of times. He threw it in the air and delivered another of his famous serves. The digital display in the corner of the court registered a hundred and fourteen miles per hour.

Max swung his racket and knocked the ball back.

Troy ran across the court, his arm outstretched, but couldn't reach the speeding ball. The crowd was silent. The umpire leaned forward, and spoke into the microphone. 'Forty-fifteen.'

Max lifted his eyes and stared at Natascha. This time, each of them gave a little smile.

Max turned around, walked to the back of the court and waited for Troy's next serve.

Chapter 17

In his hotel room, Tim was sitting on his bed, reading the autobiography of Mahatma Gandhi. Natascha had finished the book on the train back from Agra and insisted that Tim read it next.

Grk was lying on the floor, his legs twitching. He must have been dreaming.

Someone knocked on the door.

Grk sprang to his feet, the dream forgotten, and darted towards the door, barking loudly.

Tim hushed Grk, then called out, 'Who is it?'

'Room service,' replied a voice.

That's strange, thought Tim. I didn't order anything to eat. I'm not even hungry. So he shouted, 'I didn't order room service!'

'Are you Mister Tim?' said the voice.

'Yes,' said Tim.

'Then I have your room service. Will you please open the door and let me inside. Otherwise your food will get cold and tasteless and not terribly nice at all.'

They know my name, thought Tim. Dad must have ordered some food for me. Hmm, I wonder what it is. Chicken korma, perhaps. With some rice and a chapatti. And a few crunchy poppadoms too. That would be nice.

Suddenly, Tim felt hungry. He put a piece of paper in his book to keep his place, hauled himself off his bed and walked to the door. Grk followed close behind.

When Tim opened the door, he was confronted by a small boy with a big grin on his face.

'Hello, Mister Tim,' Krishnan said cheerfully. 'I am your room service!'

Tim said, 'What are you doing here?'

'I have come on a visit.'

'How did you find me?'

'Through cleverness,' said Krishnan, his grin even wider. 'Come on, please, quickly, let me inside. If the management catch me here, they will throw me right out into the street.'

Tim let Krishnan into the room and closed the door.

Grk sniffed suspiciously at Krishnan's ankles, unsure whether to trust him.

Krishnan walked into the middle of the room, looked around as if he owned the place, and nodded, fully satisfied with what he saw. 'This is very nice,' he said. 'This is indeed very nice.' He darted forward to inspect the bed, rubbing the sheets between his fingers to feel their quality. 'Oh, this is silky,' he said, his voice wistful. 'Never in my life have I slept on a sheet so silky as this.'

Tim said, 'What are you doing here? What do you want?'

'I have to ask you a question, Mister Tim. A very important question. It is a matter of life and death.'

'Whose life? Whose death?'

'The life and death of my sister,' said Krishnan. 'And

the life and death of myself too.' He walked across the room, sat down on the bed and bounced a few times, testing the springs. 'Oh, very good quality,' he said. 'This is a most excellent hotel, Mister Tim. You have chosen well.'

'I'd like to help you,' said Tim, not bothering to explain that he hadn't chosen to stay in this particular hotel, not wanting to get involved in a discussion about sheets or springs or any other aspect of the place. He simply wanted to understand why Krishnan had come to his room. 'Tell me what I can do. What's happened to your sister? Is she in danger?"

'Oh, yes. Terrible danger.'

'Why? What's happened?'

'I will tell you,' said Krishnan.

But before Krishnan could say another word, there was a knock at the door and a voice shouted, 'Room service! Room service for Mister Tim!'

Tim and Krishnan looked at one another. Neither of them moved. Both were equally confused.

Krishnan said, 'Did you order some room service?'

'No,' said Tim. 'That's why I was so surprised when you knocked on the door.'

'Then who did?'

'I don't know,' said Tim. 'But there's only one way to find out.'

Together, the two boys walked across the room, followed by Grk.

Chapter 18

Tim opened the door and found a small boy standing in the corridor. He had a big smile on his face. 'Hello, Mister Tim,' he said. 'I am here for a visit.'

'Hello,' said Tim. He recognised the boy: he had been one of Krishnan's gang at Agra railway station.

Krishnan didn't seem pleased to see his friend. He said, 'What are you doing here?'

'I am here for a visit,' said the boy. 'Just like yourself.'

'But I told you not to follow me,' said Krishnan.

The boy waggled his head and smiled. 'I am very sorry, Krishnan, but it was impossible to resist.'

Krishnan sighed. 'I have to make an apology to you, Mister Tim. Against my express instructions, this boy has followed me. Will you permit him to come inside your bedroom?'

'I suppose so,' said Tim, although he didn't really like the idea of having two strange boys in his room. What if they tried to fight him? Or attack him? Would he be able to fight them off?

Krishnan ushered the boy into the room and closed the door behind him. 'This is Arjuna,' he said. 'Please, you must meet Mister Tim.'

Arjuna placed his hands together and did a *namaste* to Tim.

Tim would have liked to do a *namaste* back again, but

he was worried that he would look stupid. So he smiled and said, 'Nice to meet you, Arjuna.'

Krishnan addressed a few words to Arjuna in Hindi, and then turned to Tim. 'Now,' he said. 'Let me tell you precisely what is happening and exactly why I am here.'

'Yes, please,' said Tim. 'I'd like that.'

Krishnan smiled. 'As soon as I saw you, Mister Tim, I knew that you are a kind man. Yes, you are a good man. A man who knows right things from wrong things. As for myself – oh, I am currently in some terrible trouble. I need your help. Please, Mister Tim, will you assist me in my time of need?'

Tim said, 'What kind of trouble are you in?'

'The most terrible trouble,' said Krishnan. 'You see, when I was—'

At that moment, there was a knock at the door and a voice shouted, 'Room service! Room service! Room service for Mister Tim!'

Krishnan, Arjuna, Tim and Grk looked at one another. All of them were equally surprised. Together, they went to the door. Tim opened it.

This time, not one but two boys were standing in the corridor. Krishnan brought them into the room and introduced them to Tim, who was beginning to lose track of all the different names.

'This is a matter for some apology,' said Krishnan. 'We have invaded the bedroom of Mister Tim. We were not invited. We were not even asked. We have been behaving like bad guests, entering the home of another man without his permission.' He turned to Tim. 'So,

Mister Tim, we must ask your apology. Will you accept?'

'I suppose so,' said Tim, wondering whether he should ask all the boys to wait outside while he finished talking to Krishnan. But what would happen if the hotel staff saw them? Or, even worse, Mr Malt? Perhaps it was safer to let them stay in the room.

But what would he do if they started to threaten him? If they tried to attack him or steal his possessions? Then he'd just have to grab the phone and call for help. He took a couple of steps backwards and made sure that he was standing near the phone, ready to lunge for it if the boys turned nasty.

But they didn't show any signs of being nasty. In fact, they were all extremely polite. One of the boys clasped his hands together and made a *namaste*. The other said, 'Thank you for your kindness, Mister Tim.'

'That's okay,' said Tim.

Krishnan had barely introduced his friends to Tim when there was another knock, then another and another and another and another, each one revealing yet another boy in the corridor. All of them came into the room and introduced themselves to Tim, smiling and doing a *namaste* and saying 'Hello' in English or Hindi and sometimes both.

Tim began to wonder if they would all fit in his bedroom. Several sat on the bed. Others squatted on the chest of drawers. More stood against the wall. A couple crouched on the floor and chatted to Grk, tickling his stomach and scratching his ears.

Grk had completely forgotten his duties as a guard dog. He just lay on the floor, wagging his tail as his tummy was tickled, looking like the happiest dog in the world.

Some of the boys were inspecting Tim's possessions, peering at his socks and his books and his toothbrush. Others were looking at the bits and pieces that had been provided by the hotel – the soap, the towels, the sheets, the pictures on the wall, the remote control for the TV – and discussing what they'd found.

Tim felt extremely uncomfortable. He didn't like having all these strangers in his room, playing with his possessions. He was just about to suggest to Krishnan that they all went somewhere else when he noticed something behind one boy's ear. A small, blueish blotch. Tim darted forwards and said to the boy, 'Would you mind if I looked at your ear?'

'No problem, Mister Tim.'

'Thanks,' said Tim. He walked behind the boy and stared at the back of his right ear. On the soft flesh which would usually be hidden from sight, there was a small blueish blotch which, if you hadn't been looking closely, you might have thought was a wart, a bruise, a birthmark or a bit of dirt. But Tim knew better. He leaned forward to get a clearer view.

Yes – there it was. The same tattoo. The same blue rat with the same long wriggly tail.

Tim looked at Krishnan. 'Do you all have them?'

'Oh, yes,' said Krishnan. 'Every one of us.'

'Let me see.'

'No problem,' said Krishnan. He clapped his hands and issued a brisk order in Hindi.

The boys gathered round. They turned their heads, pulled their right ears and displayed the undersides to Tim. Every one of them had the same tattoo in the same position on their ears.

'You have to tell me what's going on,' said Tim. 'What is this blue rat? What does it mean?'

'This is our mark,' said Krishnan.

'Your mark? Which mark?'

'I will tell you,' said Krishnan. 'I will answer every question that you wish to ask. But in order to do so, I must tell you the story of my life. It is a good story, I promise, and not too long. Will you hear it?'

When Tim agreed, Krishnan grinned. He was eager to tell his own story. He clapped his hands and issued a quick order to the other boys. They put down whatever they had been looking at – the socks, the books, the soap, the toothbrush and the remote control – and found themselves a seat somewhere in the room.

Tim sat on his bed alongside six of the boys. Grk lay on the floor alongside seven more. The remaining boys dotted themselves around the room, squatting on a bookshelf, sharing the chair or leaning with their backs to the wall.

'I was born in a village,' said Krishnan, performing to Tim, Grk and the boys like an actor performing to an audience of thousands. 'My father had been born in that village. And his father too. And his father's father.

My family had never known another place. For myself, I never thought I will know anywhere else either. And then, one day, the village was visited by the blue rat.'

Chapter 19

Inside the New Delhi Lawn Tennis Club, Max bounced the ball on the grass. He took several long, slow breaths, trying to ignore everything and everyone around him.

He was tired. He'd been playing for an hour and fifty-one minutes. Now, he needed all his skill and strength.

In a game of tennis, every point is important, but this felt like the most important point of the whole game.

The score stood at 6-3, 6–4, 5-4. If Max won this point, he would win the game, the set and the match.

Every one of Troy Crown's supporters leaned forward in their seats and roared encouragement at their hero. If he lost this point, he would lose the game, the set and the match. 'Come on, Troy,' they shouted. 'Troy! Troy! Troy! Troy is our boy! Come on, Troy!'

No one shouted for Max. No one cheered his name. He had just two supporters and both of them were too nervous to make a single sound.

Up in the stands, Natascha and Mrs Malt were sitting in their seats, holding hands, their faces white with tension. Their work was long-forgotten. Natascha had closed her notebook. Her hands were shaking so much, she couldn't even hold her pen. Mrs Malt had turned off her laptop. She hadn't written an email for the past hour. Neither of them could think of anything except the match.

'Silence, please,' said the umpire.

The crowd went quiet.

'Thank you,' said the umpire.

The court was very still.

Max bounced the ball on the grass. He took another deep breath, then tossed the ball into the air, swung his racket and served.

The ball whistled through the air, bounced once, and sped towards the back of the court, straight past Troy Crown's racket.

Troy Crown looked at the grass and blinked. He looked at his racket and blinked a second time. Then he shook his head slowly from side to side as if he was simply unable to believe what had just happened.

The crowd was silent. Not one of them moved. Six hundred people sat in their seats with their mouths open and their shoulders slumped, unable to believe that their hero had lost the game, the set and the match.

Actually, that's not quite true. One person moved. Natascha Raffifi jumped into the air, threw her hands above her head and cheered at the top of her voice.

Chapter 20

This is the story that Krishnan told.

He was born in a village where life had hardly varied for hundreds of years. Men and women worked in the fields. Their houses were small and basic. There was no glass in the windows. They had neither electricity nor running water. Every morning, women walked down to the well with buckets, returning home with enough water to get them through the rest of the day.

Once a year, the blue rat came to their village.

Krishnan's parents were farmers, but they didn't own a farm. They just worked as labourers on someone else's land. They weren't paid. Rather than getting a wage from the landowner, they were simply allowed to keep half of what they grew.

Their land belonged to the blue rat.

Krishnan's parents had six sons and five daughters. Krishnan was the fifth to be born. Most families had that many children, but several usually died before they were older than a week or two. Krishnan's brothers and sisters were exceptionally healthy. They all survived.

'I was a strong baby,' said Krishnan. 'Very big, very strong.'

He lifted his arms and showed off his muscles. The boys applauded. One jumped to his feet, wanting to show off his muscles too. Several hands grabbed the boy's clothes and pulled him backwards, forcing him to sit down again. Before the boy had a chance to protest, Krishnan continued with his story, describing what a healthy, happy baby he had been and how much his parents had loved him.

Krishnan liked having an audience. He walked up and down the room, waving his arms, making faces and using different accents for different people.

Life in the village was difficult, he said. The ground was hard. Rain was rare. Crops took a long time to grow. Every night, the whole family went to bed hungry. Every day, they worked until they were exhausted.

As soon as the children were old enough to walk, they started working too, helping their parents. One of them would watch the goats. Another pulled weeds from the fields. The elder ones carried buckets of water from the well to the house, walking slowly, taking care not to spill a single drop.

One afternoon in the spring, a truck arrived in the village.

As soon as the villagers saw a cloud of dust on the horizon, they knew that the truck was coming. They gathered in the centre of the village, waiting for the truck to arrive.

In the centre of the village, the truck shuddered to a standstill. The brakes squealed. The dust-stained wheels sent pebbles flying in every direction. The door opened and a little old woman clambered down. She looked around, staring at the villagers.

Every year, for as long as anyone could remember, this woman had come to the village with her blue rat. Everyone knew her. Everyone was terrified of her.

Trucks often came through the village. Sometimes, they carried goats or chickens, taking them from the countryside to the cities. Sometimes, they brought bricks, pipes or other building material. But the old woman's truck was carrying an entirely different cargo.

Children.

In the back of the truck, there were fifteen or twenty children. Both boys and girls. They stared at the villagers. Most of them looked too frightened to make a sound, but one was braver. He called down, begging for some water, saying that he'd die without a drink.

Krishnan's mother hurried to her house, returning with a jug of water. She handed it up to the boy. He took a drink, then passed the jug to the others. They passed it from hand to hand, taking turns to drink a few short sips.

The villagers knew what they had to do. They gathered all their children and brought them to the old woman. Every child in the village was there. No one dared disobey the blue rat.

The village's children stood in a line. The old woman looked at them, inspecting the boys and girls, as if she was trying to decide which ones to choose. She pinched their arms and inspected their teeth, trying to decide which were the strongest and healthiest.

But the old woman didn't make the final decision between the children. The blue rat did.

The blue rat crawled out of the old woman's dress,

scrambled up her body and perched on her shoulder, staring at the line of children.

Most rats are white, black or brown, but the blue rat was bright blue. It was a magical rat. A rat of great power. It had lived for fifty years, terrorising the residents of this village and many other villages, ruling over them like a lord.

Terrible things happened to anyone who disobeyed the blue rat. Their houses burned down. Their crops were destroyed. They were ambushed in the middle of the night and beaten to death. That was why the villagers did whatever the blue rat asked. Even when it demanded their children.

Now, the blue rat made its decision.

It looked up and down the line of children, inspecting their faces and bodies, then whispered its choices into the old woman's ear.

The blue rat chose two children. A boy and a girl. Krishnan and his sister.

Krishnan's mother tried not to cry. She hugged Krishnan, then his sister, and barely gave their father enough time to hug them himself before grabbing them back and gripping them with her strong arms. Tears trickled down her face. She put her mouth to Krishnan's ear and begged him to forgive her.

'We don't have any choice,' she whispered. 'There's nothing else we can do. The blue rat has chosen you.'

Krishnan and his sister pulled themselves into the back of the truck. They looked at the other children. No one smiled or said a word.

The old woman climbed into her truck. One of her men started the engine. As the truck juddered along the uneven road, Krishnan and his sister stood at the back, holding on tightly, watching the village disappear through a cloud of dust. Their mother and father stood side by side, waving, until the truck turned a corner and they were gone.

That was the last time Krishnan saw his parents.

Krishnan paused for a moment, remembering that terrible day. He sighed and shook his head, unable to continue speaking.

Immediately, several other boys started talking. Some spoke in English and others in Hindi. All of them described their homes, their villages, their families and the day that they had been forced to clamber into a truck packed with children. They too had been taken from their families by the blue rat gang.

After a minute or two, Krishnan collected himself and took control of the situation. He told the other boys to keep quiet. He was telling the story, he said, not them. He turned to Tim and picked up the story from where he had left off.

The truck drove from village to village, picking up more children.

No one dared disobey the blue rat. The old woman was allowed to take whichever children she chose.

That night, they stopped on the outskirts of a small town, where the children were fed and given rugs to sleep on.

That was Krishnan's first night away from home. It was the first time in his life that he didn't go to sleep in his own house. He huddled beside his sister. When he woke in the middle of the night, cold and scared, he had no idea where he was.

In the morning, they drove to Delhi. None of the children had ever been to a city before. They were scared by the traffic, the noises and the vast numbers of the people on the streets.

The truck stopped opposite a dark alleyway.

The children were ushered out of the truck and led down the alleyway to an old, ramshackle hut. Here, they were told to stand in a line. One by one, they went into the hut.

Inside the hut, a tattooist was sitting on the floor. When each child came in, he told them to sit down, gripped one of their ears and marked them with a tattoo of a blue rat.

Chapter 21

Tim had lots of questions, but there was only one which really mattered. He said, 'Krishnan, there's one thing about your story that I really don't understand. What's so important about this blue rat? What kind of power does it have? It's a rat, isn't it? Just a rat. Why would anyone be so frightened of a rat?'

'Oh, no,' said Krishnan. 'This is not just any old rat. This is the blue rat.'

'It's a rat that's blue?'

'That is correct.'

'But it's still a rat, right?'

'Yes.'

'So why are you scared of it? Why does anyone do what it wants?'

'Because the blue rat is a rat of great power.'

'I don't understand,' said Tim. 'What power can a rat have?'

'The power to kill you, for instance. The power to destroy your home. The power to understand what you are thinking, even. You see, Mister Tim, the blue rat is no ordinary rat. The blue rat is like a god. A very, very bad god.'

'That's crazy,' said Tim. 'Rats don't have power. Not even blue rats.'

'Perhaps not in your country,' said Krishnan. 'But

things are different here. In India, the blue rat is very, very powerful. As I told you already, he has the power of a god.'

Tim sighed. He didn't understand what was going on. Why would anyone be scared of a rat? Why would anyone give away their children just because a rat told them to? His parents might have been annoying in all sorts of ways, but they wouldn't give him away. Not to a blue rat or an old woman or anyone else.

Reminded of his parents, he glanced at the clock on the bedside table. It was getting late. It was time to stop arguing and clear the nineteen boys out of his room. He said, 'Look, my mum and dad will be back soon. If they find you all here, they'll go nuts. I think you should go.'

Krishnan smiled. 'Yes, of course, Mister Tim. We will go now. Thank you for your time. So, shall we say nine o'clock?'

'What do you mean?'

'At nine o'clock tomorrow morning, I will come here for picking you up. We will meet outside the hotel. Is that a good time? Or would you prefer me to come at ten?'

'Picking me up? What are you talking about?'

'To bring you to the factory.'

'Why?'

'To save my sister from the blue rat.'

'How am I going to save your sister from the blue rat?'

Krishnan rolled his eyes as if Tim was being ridiculously slow. 'I have already explained to you, Mister Tim. This is why I am here. Because I need your help. I cannot fight the blue rat without your help. I need you to come to the factory and save our skins.'

'Me? What can I do? I'm just a boy. How can I help?'

'I saw what you did to Gunyan,' said Krishnan. 'You stood up to him. You may be just a boy but you talked to him like a man. That was when I knew. You are the one to save us.'

'I can't save you,' said Tim. 'I don't know anything about you. I don't know anything about India either. I can't speak Hindi. I've never been here before. Look, I've got a much better idea. Rather than asking me for help, why don't you go to the police?'

As soon as Tim said that word, all the other boys started talking loudly in English and Hindi, and Krishnan shook his head. 'Oh, no. Not possible. No police.'

'Why not?'

'Oh, Mister Tim, the police is very bad people. I don't want to have a broken head. Any more than you do.'

'I don't think the police would break my head,' said Tim.

'Okay, maybe there will be no head-breaking for you. Because you're a tourist. But they will definitely break my head. Look, you see this?' Krishnan turned round, pulled up his T-shirt and showed Tim a long scar running along the skin of his back. 'One policeman did that. Yes, truly. He cut me with his knife.'

'When?'

'Two years ago. I was working in New Delhi Station. The police came and made a big attack. They kick us, they hit us, they cut me with their knife. You see? They do this to me.'

Tim was shocked. 'But why? Why would the police want to hurt you like that?'

'This is India,' said Krishnan. 'This is what happens here. If you are rich, you are happy and life is good. But if you are a poor boy, then life is very, very bad.'

Before Tim could ask another question or even say another word, the other boys crowded round, showing wounds that they too had received at the hands of the police.

Krishnan clapped his hands together, calling for silence.

When the other boys had finally stopped talking, Krishnan turned to Tim and said, 'Mister Tim, the moment has arrived for us to go. We cannot take up any more of your valuable time. But first, I must ask you one question. You know everything. All our troubles. All our problems. And this is what I must ask you. Will you help me? Will you help my sister? Will you fight the blue rat for us? What is your answer, Mister Tim? Yes or no?'

Chapter 22

When Tim didn't know what to do, there were always two people whose opinions he asked.

The first of these people wasn't exactly a person. Their conversations weren't exactly conversations. Even so, Tim always liked talking to Grk – or rather, talking *at* Grk, because Grk never said a single word back again.

However, there are times when you need to talk to someone who can actually reply. At those times, Tim liked to talk to Natascha.

There were other people whose opinions he could have asked. His parents, for instance. Or Max. But he didn't want to bother Max, whose attention was completely taken up by the tennis tournament. And he didn't really trust his parents. If he told them that his room had been invaded by nineteen Indian boys begging for his help in their battle against the blue rat gang, they probably wouldn't have let him out of their sight until the day that they left India and flew back home.

No, there was only one person whose opinion he wanted to ask, and that person was Natascha.

He didn't get a chance till later that night. Whenever Tim tried to take Natascha aside and have a private word with her, one of his parents always seemed to be nearby, discussing the tennis, the Taj Mahal or the menu for that night's supper. Tim didn't want to be overheard. This conversation was strictly private. In the end, Tim simply said, 'I'm taking Grk for a walk. Round the hotel garden. I think he needs a pee. Does anyone else want to come too?' To his relief, Natascha was the only person who said yes.

The three of them strolled through the hotel's gardens. Strong, sweet scents floated on the warm air. Bats fluttered overhead. Grk darted from tree to tree, having a pee under each one, leaving his mark and alerting other dogs to his presence.

Tim still had to wait quite a long time before getting a chance to discuss the dilemma that he was facing. First, Natascha insisted on telling him all about the day's tennis, describing exactly how Max had beaten Troy Crown and progressed to the second round of the tournament. Tomorrow afternoon, he would play a boy named Mustafa Myrtle.

When Natascha had finished describing the highs and lows of Max's triumph, she said, 'How about you? What was your day like? Did anything exciting happen?'

'My room was invaded by nineteen boys,' said Tim, 'who asked me to help them defeat the leader of the blue rat gang.'

'Very funny,' said Natascha. 'What did you really do all day?'

Tim told her that he wasn't joking. He described the unexpected arrival of nineteen scruffy boys and the way that they had taken over his room. He described a few of them, recalling their names, the clothes that they had worn and the stories that they had told. He explained everything, describing how he had found Krishnan in Agra, what Krishnan had revealed of his own life and the desperate plea that Krishnan had made, begging for Tim's help.

As Tim talked, the mocking smile faded from Natascha's face. Realising that he was telling the truth, she listened in silence.

When Tim finished talking, Natascha stood in silence for a few moments, thinking about what he had said. Finally, she asked, 'So, what are you going to do?'

'I don't know,' said Tim. 'Krishnan said he'd wait for me tomorrow morning. He'll be outside the hotel at nine o'clock. I just have to decide whether to go and meet him.'

'What would happen if you didn't?'

'I guess he'd just wait there till he realised I wasn't coming. Then he'd go away again.'

'And if you do go and meet him?'

'He's going to take me to the factory. And when we get there...I don't really know. He wants me to help him and all the other children in the factory. But I don't know what I can do. I can't stop the blue rat gang. I can't free Krishnan and his sister from slavery. They need the police. Or someone with lots of money and power. Not me.'

Natascha said, 'Do they believe in the blue rat?'

'I don't know.'

'Do they think it has power over them?'

'Yes, I suppose so. They're certainly scared of it. If it told them to do something, they'd do it.'

'Then it does have power over them,' said Natascha. 'That's what power is. If you can persuade other people to do what you want, then you've got power over them.'

They walked round the garden in silence. Although Tim felt a bit impatient, he trusted Natascha. She usually had good ideas. If he kept quiet and let her think, she'd probably come up with a cunning plan.

They had been walking for about twenty minutes in complete silence when Natascha turned to Tim with a triumphant smile. 'Got it!' she said. 'I know exactly what we should do!'

Tim noticed that she had said 'we' rather than 'you', but he didn't mind. Actually, he was pleased. If he was going to spend tomorrow morning on a secret mission, sneaking into an illegal factory and breaking up the blue rat gang, he'd much rather do it with her than on his own. So he just said, 'What are we going to do?'

'Krishnan can take us to the factory tomorrow morning and we'll write an article about it.'

'An article?' said Tim. 'What kind of article?'

'An exposé of the appalling working conditions in one of India's factories. Showing how children are abused by evil employers.'

'But we're not journalists. We can't just write an article.'

'Of course we can,' said Natascha. 'We can write better than most journalists. I can, anyway, and that's what matters. Because I'm the one who's going to write it.'

'And what am I going to do?'

'You're going to take the pictures.'

Chapter 23

It was another bright, hot morning in Delhi. The sun was shining and parrots were chirruping in the palm trees. Mrs Malt was sitting in one of the hotel's restaurants, her fingers poised over the keys of her laptop. She had slept well and was now ready to work hard. Before she started, there was just one thing to do: she had to make sure that the children weren't going to get bored, lonely or lost.

She looked at the two children standing before her and said, 'Are you sure you don't mind looking after yourselves this morning?'

'I'm sure I'm sure,' said Tim.

'Me too,' said Natascha.

Grk wagged his tail.

'That's such a help,' said Mrs Malt. 'I'm just so busy today. I've got to finish this report by lunchtime. And your father is completely frantic too. Oh, I wish things were different. I wish I could just spend the day with you. You're absolutely sure you don't mind?'

'We don't mind at all,' said Tim.

'We'll be fine,' said Natascha.

Grk wagged his tail again.

'That's so helpful of you both,' said Mrs Malt. 'So, what are you going to do now? Do you think you'll be able to find some way to entertain yourselves?'

'We'll just wander round the hotel,' said Tim. He lifted up his camera, which was attached to his wrist on a short string. 'I'd like to take some more photos.'

'I'd like to buy some souvenirs,' said Natascha. She was holding her journal and a couple of pens. 'And maybe send some postcards to some people at school.'

Mrs Malt smiled. 'That sounds perfect. But you won't leave the hotel, will you?'

'No, Mum,' said Tim.

'Of course not,' said Natascha.

Mrs Malt said, 'You promise?'

'I promise,' said Tim.

'Me too,' said Natascha.

Grk wagged his tail once more.

Mrs Malt's computer beeped. She glanced at the screen of her laptop. An email had arrived. 'Have a lovely day,' she said, giving a quick wave to the children, then peering at the screen and reading the first few words of the email.

Tim and Natascha walked away from her table and headed through the restaurant towards the exit. Grk trotted at their feet, looking around and impatiently sniffing the air, eager to get going.

Although they had never even considered telling Mrs Malt what they were really doing or where they were really going, they would have liked to tell Max. On any other day, they would have done so. But they knew that today, Max wouldn't want to be disturbed by anyone or anything. He had other things to worry about. His match was scheduled for half past four. Before that, he was planning to relax, do some gentle exercise and think through his tactics.

Natascha was determined to see Max's match. She had to be sitting in her seat inside the tennis court by four o'clock. So they had seven hours to break into the factory, gather evidence that would condemn the blue rat gang, then get out again and make their way to the tennis courts.

They went through the lobby and out of the big glass doors. Outside, the bright sun was blinding, so they couldn't immediately see the small boy who was waiting for them.

'Over here!' yelled Krishnan. 'Here! Here! Mister Tim, over here!'

Krishnan was sitting on the saddle of a cycle rickshaw. He jumped to the ground and hurried forward to greet Tim. 'I am so very pleased to see you, Mister Tim. In my head, a little voice has been saying, maybe he will not come. But a big voice was saying, do not be so ridiculous, of course he will come. Mister Tim is a good man, says the big voice. He always does what he says he will do. And you see! Here you are! My big voice was right.' Krishnan clasped his hands, palms together, and did a *namaste*.

Tim did the same thing back again. The gesture felt a bit odd, but he was getting used to it. He said, 'This is Natascha. She's going to come too.'

'Any friend of Mister Tim is a friend of mine,' said Krishnan. He turned to look at Natascha, then grinned, recognising her from the train. 'Oh, yes. We have met on a previous occasion. You are the Harry Potter girl, yes?'

'If you mean that I bought a copy of Harry Potter from you, then I am,' said Natascha. 'But I have to say, it wasn't a good copy of Harry Potter. It had several pages upside down. And several more pages missing. You cheated me, didn't you?'

'I am very sorry,' said Krishnan. 'But this is my business. Selling bad books. Stealing from tourists. Cheating the visitors to our country. Doing bad things. This is why you must help me. You must make me a good man. An honest man. You must save me from the life of badness and make me good again. Am I right, Mister Tim?'

'I hope so,' said Tim.

'So,' said Krishnan. 'How are you going to save me?'

'I'll tell you,' said Tim. Quickly, he explained Natascha's plan. He showed Krishnan his camera, with which he was planning to take photos of the factory, and explained how Natascha was intending to write an article describing what they saw.

Krishnan clapped his hands with delight. 'This is a very fine plan! When the good people of your country know about the bad things happening here in Delhi, they will save us all. Ah, Mister Tim, you are a very, very clever man.'

'Actually, it was Natascha's idea, not mine.'

'Very, very clever and very, very modest!' Krishnan clapped his hands again. 'Mister Tim, you have the perfect combination!'

Before Tim could protest any more, Natascha reminded him that they had to hurry. She explained to Krishnan that her brother was playing a very important tennis match at half past four and it was vital that she reached the New Delhi Lawn Tennis Club at least half an hour in advance. Max always played better when she was watching. If she missed the match, he might lose.

'Then we must be going in double-quick time,' said Krishnan. He ushered the three of them into the back of the rickshaw.

When Tim and Natascha were sitting comfortably on the padded cushions, with Grk squeezed between them, Krishnan pushed the rickshaw forwards.

The wheels started rolling. The entire structure wobbled from side to side, threatening to topple over or throw the three passengers overboard. Tim and Natascha held on tight.

Krishnan hopped into the saddle, placed his hands on the handlebars and his feet on the pedals, and started cycling.

Chapter 24

The rickshaw was much too big for Krishnan. His feet barely reached the pedals. But he didn't seem daunted. He cycled fast, his frantic energy more than compensating for his short legs.

Every pothole threatened to throw his passengers into the road. Every car, bus and lorry represented the threat of a terrible accident. Krishnan needed all his skill, courage and strength to steer a safe course through the lines of speeding traffic.

As the rickshaw swayed violently from side to side, Tim and Natascha clung to the armrests, praying that none of the thundering trucks or lumbering buses would run them down.

Grk was tucked cosily between Tim and Natascha, but he didn't look cosy at all. In fact, he looked thoroughly miserable. His eyes were half-closed and his ears were lying flat against his skull.

In his short life, Grk had travelled by plane, train, car, boat, scooter, bicycle and helicopter, but this was his first time in a cycle-rickshaw. Judging by his expression, he wasn't impressed.

The sun was hot. The air was thick with pollution. When Krishnan stopped pedalling and rolled the rickshaw to a halt by the side of the road, Tim assumed he must be stopping for a rest.

Sweat was pouring down Krishnan's forehead. He was breathing heavily. The interior of his lungs must have been coated with black dust and smog and smoke and all the other nasty substances that gush out of the back of cars, buses and trucks.

Krishnan didn't seem to care. He wasn't even tired. He sprang off the saddle, pushed his hand into his pocket and pulled out a blue pen. 'It is time for the tattooing. Please, hold still your heads.'

Grk struggled to his feet and tensed his muscles, preparing to leap down from the rickshaw and regain the safety of solid ground.

Just in time, Tim grabbed his collar. 'No, no. You're staying here. We haven't arrived yet.'

With a sad sigh, Grk lay down again, propping his head on Natascha's knee. She tickled his ears, which usually put him in a good mood, but Grk refused to cheer up. He was determined to stay miserable until he was allowed to get out of the rickshaw.

Using his blue pen, Krishnan drew a tiny rat behind Tim's right ear, then Natascha's. He was a good artist. The tattoos looked exactly like his.

Krishnan glanced at Grk, considering whether he needed a tattoo behind his ear too, but Grk's expression convinced him not to bother. An hour's rattling ride in the back of the rickshaw had put Grk in such a bad mood that anyone who came near him risked getting their fingers bitten off. 'The dog is fine,' said Krishnan, who wanted to keep all his fingers. 'No need for tattooing him. Let's be going now. Just around the corner, we will find the factory.'

Natascha said, 'Are there guards?'

'Of course there are guards,' said Krishnan.

'What happens if they catch us?'

'They will beat you with sticks. Oh, it will be very painful. But we will not be caught.'

'How do you know?'

'What are all these questions? I thought you were in a hurry!' With a cheeky grin, Krishnan swung himself back onto the saddle and started pedalling.

As the rickshaw plunged into the traffic, drivers yelled abuse, horns hooted, brakes screeched and cars swerved, but Krishnan took no notice. He had more important things to worry about. His legs whirred, turning the pedals, forcing the rickshaw's wheels to roll faster and faster over the uneven ground. He steered through a narrow alleyway, emerged in a wide road, turned a corner, then another, and finally rolled to a standstill beside four other cycle-rickshaws.

A boy was already running towards them. He had black hair and angry eyes. Shrieking with fury, he grabbed the handlebars from Krishnan, then gestured at Tim and Natascha, ordering them to climb down from the rickshaw. 'Get out!' he shouted. 'Get out! You must now get out!'

As soon as Tim and Natascha had clambered down from the seat at the back, and Grk had gratefully leaped to the ground, the boy swung himself into the saddle. Without a backward glance, he started pedalling away.

By lending his rickshaw to Krishnan, he had missed a whole morning's work. He would have to carry passengers late into the night to make up for the money that he had lost.

'This way,' said Krishnan, pushing through the crowd and urging Tim and Natascha to follow.

Although they had only been standing in the same spot for half a minute, a mob had already gathered. People had come from all directions to see what was going on. Dogs came too, attracted by Grk's smell, wanting to know who this strange dog was and why he smelled so different. Even a piglet had wandered across to have a look at Tim and Natascha, snuffling the muddy ground around their feet, searching for nice scraps of food.

People hurled questions at Krishnan. They wanted to know why Tim and Natascha had come here. Who were these two children? Were they foreigners? Tourists? From which country? Were they rich? What did they want? And why had they brought a dog?

Batting aside all these questions, Krishnan led the children through the crowd. 'Come on,' he said. 'This way. We have to go.' Holding Tim with one hand and Natascha with the other, he pushed past people, ignoring their protests, and led the way down a dark alleyway which led into the slums. A few stragglers tried to follow them, but Krishnan angrily waved them away.

The four of them walked quickly down the alleyway. Tim would have liked to take some photos, Natascha wanted to write some notes and Grk sensed the presence

111

of a hundred different fascinating smells, but the three of them didn't have a chance to take a single sniff, note or photo. They were moving too fast.

After a couple of minutes, Krishnan stopped beside the entrance to a dark, shadowy alleyway. The ground was damp. The walls were mouldy. He said, 'Now, you must be quiet. When we meet the guards, you don't talk. I talk, not you. Okey-dokey?'

Tim and Natascha nodded.

Krishnan said, 'Also, you must be staying with me all the time. No running away. If you are getting lost, you will be lost to the end of your days. Okey-dokey?'

'Fine,' said Natascha.

'Sure,' said Tim.

Grk wagged his tail.

'Good,' said Krishnan. 'Then you must follow me. Let us be going inside.'

He led them down the alleyway and into the factory.

Chapter 25

The factory looked unlike any factory that Tim or Natascha had ever seen. There wasn't a single chimney, for instance. There weren't even any big buildings. It didn't really look like a factory at all, but just a bunch of small, rickety shacks which housed people who couldn't afford to live anywhere better.

And that's exactly what it was. The factory was in one of the most decrepit slums in the city. Only the very poorest citizens of Delhi lived here. The walls of the run-down shacks were built of mud or old bricks which had been discarded or stolen from other buildings. The roofs were made from corrugated iron or plastic sheeting. On rainy days, half the residents woke up to find bits of their homes had been washed away. A big storm would have blown down the whole place.

From the outside, no one would have guessed the presence of the factory. There were no gates. No uniformed guards checked the identities of visitors. Anyone could walk inside. And so no one did. By looking so shabby, the slum served as the perfect hiding place for a secret factory.

As soon as they entered the alleyway, everything changed. Strong smells overwhelmed their senses. Open drains ran down the middle of the narrow lanes between the houses, flowing with all kinds of stinking junk. The air grew cooler. Overlapping roofs shaded the slums from the sun's strong heat. The noise of traffic faded, replaced by the voices of humans and the cries of animals. No cars, lorries or buses could fit through these narrow streets.

Families of cats and dogs dozed in doorways. A big white cow stood in the middle of the alleyway, nuzzling a pile of rubbish.

After a few paces, Natascha and Tim were lost, bewildered by the constant twists and turns of the alleyway, but Krishnan knew exactly where he was going. He walked fast, never pausing, never stopping to consider which way he should go. The others had to move quickly to keep up with him. Grk was panting. He tried to stop and drink from a muddy puddle, but Tim tugged his lead, not wanting to get left behind.

If they hadn't been moving so fast, they might have heard the sound of approaching footsteps. They could have turned back or hidden. But there wasn't time. They saw the guards at exactly the same moment that the guards saw them.

All three guards looked strong and vicious. They were wearing black trousers, black boots and black shirts, and were carrying long bamboo canes. On a dark night, they would have blended into the shadows.

The man in the middle, the tallest and broadest of the three, barked a question at Krishnan in Hindi. The other two guards raised their canes, ready to bring them crashing down on the children's heads.

114

Tim and Natascha tensed. They didn't know what to do. Had they been caught? Should they turn and run? If so, which way?

Down on the ground, Grk opened his mouth. He didn't have any questions. He didn't want to run. He was just preparing himself to dart forward and dig his teeth in the ankles of these three aggressive men.

Krishnan was the only one who had a cool, calm reaction. With a quiet smile on his face, he stepped forward and replied to the three men, speaking Hindi as they had done.

These two foreigners come from London, explained Krishnan. They are members of the London branch of the blue rat gang. They have come here to inspect our work.

When the guards protested, saying that they had never heard of a London branch of the gang, Krishnan asked both Tim and Natascha to pin back their right ears and show the blue rats that had been tattooed there.

If any of the guards had thought of licking their fingers and rubbing the tattoos, they could have washed them away. Luckily, all of them were immediately convinced that Krishnan was telling the truth. Treating Tim and Natascha like honoured guests, they bowed and ushered them onwards, down another dark alleyway, deeper into the slum.

Krishnan led them on a circuitous route, turning left, then right, then left again, weaving through narrow alleyways, keeping his visitors hidden from curious eyes. Almost immediately, Tim and Natascha lost all sense of direction. Neither of them had any idea which way they had come from. Only Grk would have been able to find his way back again, using his sensitive nose to retrace the scent that they had laid.

Natascha stopped. She grabbed Tim's arm and pointed. 'Look,' she whispered.

Up ahead, there was a small dark shape moving slowly across the mud, snuffling at the puddles with its pointed nose. It was a black rat.

Tim and Natascha glanced at one another. Neither of them liked rats.

Grk opened his mouth and growled. He didn't like rats either.

Hearing Grk's growl, the rat turned its head and gave him a good long stare. It didn't seem to be scared of Grk. Nor did it care that three children were standing nearby. The rat just sniffed the air, as if it was deciding whether they were worth further investigation, and then must have decided that they weren't. Turning its back on them, the rat scurried through a puddle and disappeared into one of the huts.

Natascha whispered, 'Are you okay?'

'Sure,' said Tim, although he wasn't really. The sight of the black rat had made him want to run straight out of the slum. He didn't mind dirt or darkness, but rats terrified him. Nevertheless, he tried to smile and sound brave. 'This is interesting,' he said. 'How about you? Are you okay?'

'Oh, I'm fine,' whispered Natascha. 'We don't want to give up now. Do we?'

'Definitely not,' whispered Tim. 'We're here now. We can't turn round.'

Each of them knew that the other wasn't really telling the truth. They both would have been happy to turn round, go back to the hotel and spend a few hours wandering through the corridors or lazing beside the pool. Running away from your parents sounds fun. Arriving in a smelly slum is a lot less fun. Diving deeper and deeper into the slum's darkness isn't fun at all – especially when you have no idea where you're going or what you'll find when you get there.

Down on the ground, Grk wasn't frightened at all. He was sniffing the air, intrigued by all the different smells, and his tail was slowly wagging from side to side. This was much more interesting than the hotel, which just smelled of soap and floor polish. He pulled at the lead, wanting to keep walking and exploring.

'No time for chitchat,' said Krishnan, lifting his right arm and wagging his finger at them. 'What is all this dawdling? We have places to go and people to see.'

'Lead the way,' said Natascha. 'We're ready.'

Krishnan hurried onwards. The others followed him. They walked quickly through the apparently endless alleyways.

When they reached a large, low shack, built from crumbling bricks, Krishnan stopped. 'Here is the factory,' he said.

'I thought we were already in the factory,' said Tim.

'Yes, yes. *This* is the factory,' said Krishnan, gesturing all around him at the walls and roofs and alleyways of the slum. 'And also *this*' – he pointed through the doorway – 'is the factory.'

'I don't understand,' said Tim.

'You will. When you see inside. Come on, follow me.' Krishnan stepped forward, ducked under a low doorway and disappeared into the darkness.

Tim and Natascha glanced at one another. They were both scared. Neither of them could hide that fact from the other. But there was no turning back now. Not having come this far. They had to go inside.

Tim stepped forward. Grk trotted after him. Natascha came last. One by one, they entered the factory.

Chapter 26

When his eyes had adjusted to the gloom, Tim realised that he was standing in a small room barely bigger than his own bedroom. But the contents of this shack were very different from the contents of his bedroom. In place of a bed, a wardrobe and a bookshelf, there was no furniture at all, just twenty girls sitting cross-legged on the ground, working quickly and quietly, folding sheets of printed paper and stuffing them into rectangular plastic cases.

The children weren't the only occupants of the room. There were three black rats too, scampering across the floor, treating the room as if it belonged to them. None of the children seemed to be concerned by the presence of the rats. They didn't shoo them away. Even when the rats touched them, running over their hands or legs, they didn't react, as if they had grown entirely accustomed to sharing their space with small, furry, four-legged creatures.

The longer that Tim stood there, looking at the room, the more rats he saw. There were four. No, five. Six! Seven! Eight! Nine! Ten! Turning his head from side to side, Tim tried to keep count, but it was impossible. As soon as he thought that he'd counted them all, he saw another, then another, muddling him completely until he forgot which ones he had already counted.

Grk strained on his lead and growled softly. He wanted to chase the rats and clear them out of the room. Rats are usually scared of dogs, but these ones weren't. That made Grk even more anxious to attack them.

Whatever happened in a fight between Grk and the rats, the outcome would be messy. Tim took a firm grip on Grk's lead and pulled him closer.

Krishnan darted forward and picked up one of the plastic cases. He handed it to Tim. 'You see? For movie.'

Tim inspected the case. It was a box for a DVD. There wasn't a disc inside, but the colourful cover advertised a recent Hollywood movie. He said, 'Where's the DVD?'

'Another room. We will see it in one minute.'

Natascha tugged Krishnan's sleeve to get his attention. 'Can we take photos? And write notes?'

'Yes, yes,' said Krishnan. 'Please, you must record all this information for the newspapers.'

Natascha opened her notebook and scribbled some notes on what she could see. Tim snapped several photos. He wanted to take a good picture of the rats and the children together, but the children never stopped working and the rats never stopped moving.

Every few minutes, another child or two came into the room. Most were girls, although there were a few young boys too. Some arrived with more empty cases and more paper needing to be folded. Others removed piles of finished cases, taking them to the next part of the factory, where they would be filled with DVDs. It was like an assembly line; each group of children created a different part of the final product.

'Come,' said Krishnan. 'We see more. Follow me.'

He led them out of the shack. They hopped over a stinking stream, ducked under a doorway and went into another shack. Here, thirty more children were squatting on the floor, fitting DVDs into plastic cases, matching the disc to the cover. Every minute or two, another child hurried in or out of the door. Some brought cases and discs to be put together. Others carried piles of finished DVDs. Each of them was an integral part of the assembly line. In a more modern factory, machinery would have done all these jobs. Here, there weren't any machines; there were just children.

Krishnan waited until Tim had photographed everything and Natascha had scrawled several pages of notes, then led them to several more shacks. In one, a machine was printing hundreds and hundreds of books. In another, children were fitting CDs into plastic boxes. In the next, several printers were churning out colourful covers to be fitted on the books, CDs and DVDs.

Krishnan explained how the whole process worked. It was very straightforward. Someone would steal or buy a book, CD or DVD. They would bring it to the factory, where it would be fed into a computer, then printed and reproduced thousands of times. Each original CD, DVD or book might cost a few hundred rupees, but it could be used to create an infinite number of copies, which wouldn't cost more than ten or twenty rupees to make. The new CD, DVD or book would be given a cover, then taken into the streets by yet more children and sold for much less than the original.

Both Tim and Natascha had lots of questions about the process, the profits and the people who worked in the factory, but Krishnan didn't want to answer any of them. 'Less talking, more walking,' he said. 'We must meet my sister. She is not far. Come now, follow me.'

Chapter 27

Krishnan led them out of the shack and down the alley. Natascha hurried alongside him, asking questions and writing his responses in her notebook. Tim followed behind, taking photos of anything interesting that he noticed: two little girls carrying boxes of books; a skinny boy weighed down by a big wooden crate packed with DVDs; a discarded computer, smashed in half, lying in a puddle in the middle of an alleyway.

If Tim had wanted to take photos of rats, he could have taken hundreds. They were everywhere, scuffling through the mud, gnawing on wood and plastic, going about their business as if the slum belonged to them rather than to the humans.

Although the rats seemed completely uninterested in Tim, many did stop and look at Grk, giving him a good long stare and sniffing the air a few times, getting a measure of his scent, before continuing with their business. For some reason, they seemed completely confident that the small dog wouldn't or couldn't attack them. Perhaps they could see he was tied to his owner on a lead. More likely, they knew he couldn't overcome them all. One small dog could certainly kill one rat, probably two and perhaps even three, but what could he do against ten? Or twenty? Or even a hundred? As soon as he got his teeth stuck into one, ninety-nine more would swarm over his body, pinning him to the ground and biting him with their own small, sharp teeth. Against such an army of rats, Grk didn't stand a chance.

They had been walking for a few minutes when Krishnan stopped and held up his hand for silence. 'Here is more danger,' he whispered, speaking so quietly that the others had to lean forward to hear him. 'These guards know me. They know my sister also. If they see me with you, there is big, big problem. So we must be quiet. Okey-dokey?'

Tim and Natascha nodded. Neither of them said a word.

Down on the ground, Grk glanced from Krishnan to Tim to Natascha, then back again. He didn't make a sound. He understood the importance of keeping quiet.

From that point onwards, Krishnan went slowly, pausing at every intersection and listening for approaching footsteps. The others followed close behind him, never saying a word. Natascha kept her notebook shut. Tim didn't take a single photo.

Their caution was soon rewarded. Krishnan lifted his right hand, halting them. He was listening carefully. Neither Tim nor Natascha could hear anything, but Krishnan's hearing must have been more acute than theirs, because he suddenly ducked into a dark doorway and beckoned for them to follow him. There was just enough time to huddle into the shadows, hidden from sight, when a group of four guards came marching down the alleyway.

The four men were wearing black shirts, black trousers and shiny black boots. Each of them was carrying a bamboo cane. The man at the front, the leader, had a pistol tucked into his belt. They were walking fast, intent on getting to their destination, and didn't bother glancing to either side, which was why they failed to see the three children and the dog.

Krishnan waited until the sound of their footsteps had faded before emerging from the doorway. He looked both ways. He listened. Finally satisfied that the guards had gone and no more were coming, he beckoned to Tim, Natascha and Grk. 'Let's go,' he whispered. 'Not far now.'

He led them onwards, down one alley, round a corner and down another, and then stopped them again. He put his finger to his lips, telling them to be quiet, and crept forward.

Imitating Krishnan and following just behind him, Tim and Natascha pressed themselves against the wall and crept towards the end of the alleyway until they could see round the corner.

Two guards were marching past. If either of them had glanced to the left, they would have seen three children and a dog lurking in the shadows, but they were both too absorbed in their argument to look at anything except one another. They were discussing the current state of Indian cricket. Each of them knew exactly what was wrong with the national team and how it could be put right.

Both of them were wearing the uniform of all the factory's guards – a black shirt, black trousers and black boots – but, rather than the heavy wooden stick that the other guards carried, these two had pistols in leather holsters slung around their shoulders.

When the guards had gone past, waving their arms and angrily discussing the merits of different batsmen, Krishnan pointed to a dark doorway directly opposite. 'My sister is in there,' he whispered.

Tim whispered, 'How do we get inside?'

'We run.'

'But how?'

'Like this,' whispered Krishnan. He glanced at the guards, checking that their backs were still turned, then dashed across the alleyway. If either of the guards had happened to turn round, they couldn't have failed to see him, but they were so absorbed in their argument that they didn't even hear his footsteps.

On the other side of the alleyway, Krishnan leaped through the doorway and disappeared into the darkness.

When you have to do something scary, it's always best to do it fast. Then you don't have time to worry about how scared you are. Following Krishnan, Tim sprinted out of the shadows, darted across the alleyway and ducked through the dark doorway. Grk ran after him. Natascha came last.

Just as Natascha was hurling herself into the doorway, the guards turned round. One of them didn't see a thing.

The other glimpsed a flash of movement. He shouted a warning to his colleague.

All thoughts of cricket forgotten, the two guards pulled their pistols from their holsters and sprinted down the alleyway.

Chapter 28

As soon as Krishnan entered the shack, twenty girls lifted their heads from the clothes that they were sewing and started talking to him, saying hello or asking questions. They all knew him and liked him. He came here almost every day to visit his sister.

When he was followed by a boy, a dog and a girl, leaping through the doorway in swift succession, their questions got louder and more insistent, but none of them received an answer. Krishnan snapped a quick order in Hindi, telling them to be quiet and reminding them about the guards. Taking no chances, Krishnan pushed Tim and Natascha to the floor, covered them with a pile of clothes, and threw himself after them. Just in time, Grk jumped under the pile too.

'Lie still,' hissed Krishnan. 'No moving.'

A moment later, one of the guards came through the door. He swivelled round the room, pointing his pistol at each of the girls in turn, and said, 'What's happening? What's going on? What's all the noise about?'

One of the smallest girls answered him. She was only six years old and her face had the innocence of an angel. 'Nothing's happening,' she said. 'We were just singing.'

'Singing? Why?'

'Because it's my birthday today.'

No one would have believed that a girl with such a sweet, innocent face was capable of lying. Nevertheless, the guard looked around the shack, checking for signs of anything unusual, but everything looked normal. Satisfied, he said, 'Happy birthday.'

'Thank you, sir,' said the little girl.

The guard tucked his pistol into his holster and went outside again. His colleague was waiting for him. Together, the two guards resumed their constant march up and down the alleyway, searching for intruders.

One of the girls nudged Krishnan, letting him know that the guard had gone. He poked his head out of the pile of clothes and stayed still for a moment, listening to the footsteps in the alleyway. Satisfied that the guards were absorbed in their conversation about cricket, Krishnan helped Tim and Natascha to their feet.

As if this was a signal for them to stop working, twenty girls dropped their needles and thread on the floor, and hurried forward, fascinated by these two foreign children and their little white dog.

Before they even had a chance to start talking, Krishnan hushed them. Any unusual sounds would bring both guards rushing back inside to find out what was happening – and, this time, they wouldn't be satisfied with some story about a birthday.

Some of the girls reached forward, touching Tim's clothes or stroking Natascha's arm, whispering to them in languages that they couldn't understand. Others kneeled on the ground and talked to Grk in a language that he spoke perfectly – the language of cuddling and tickling.

Krishnan introduced one of the girls as his sister. She was a small, frail-looking girl with a pretty smile. She raised her hands in a *namaste* and said, 'Hello, nice meet you. My name is Karishma.'

'Hello, Karishma,' said Natascha. 'It's nice to meet you too. What do you do here?'

'Clothes. Make clothes.'

'What kind of clothes?'

'I show you.' Karishma smiled and hurried to the other side of the room.

While she was gone, Krishnan explained that Karishma couldn't speak much English. While Krishnan was travelling on the train from Agra to Delhi and back again, spending his days chatting to tourists, Karishma stayed inside the factory, working with these other girls, speaking only to them. Lacking the opportunity to practise, she hadn't learned more than a few words of basic English.

'I have been trying to teach her more of your English words,' said Krishnan. 'It is the most useful language for getting ahead in the world.'

Karishma returned with a bundle of clothes and showed them what she had made: perfect copies of expensive clothes, labelled with the motifs of exclusive designers. If these blouses, skirts, shirts and trousers had been authentic, they would have cost hundreds of pounds.

'These are beautiful,' said Natascha, spreading out a

Prada blouse and a pair of Versace trousers. She looked at Tim. 'Don't you think so?'

'I guess,' said Tim, shrugging his shoulders. He wasn't interested in fashion. He recognised the names on some of the labels – Gucci, Armani, Tommy Hilfiger – but he didn't understand what was so special about them. To him, they just looked like clothes.

Krishnan said, 'You want?'

'Really?' Natascha looked at the Prada blouse in her hands. 'I can keep it?'

'Yes, yes,' said Krishnan. 'It is a present. From me and my sister to you.'

'Thank you,' said Natascha. 'Thank you, Krishnan. Thank you, Karishma.' She slipped her arms into the blouse and put it on over her T-shirt.

'Beautiful,' said Krishnan. 'Oh, this is beautiful.'

Natascha did a little twirl. She looked at Tim. 'What do you think?'

'Very nice,' said Tim. 'Bit big, though.'

'I'll grow into it.'

Krishnan said, 'So, Mister Tim, what will you have? One shirt? One jacket?'

'I'm fine, thanks,' said Tim. 'I don't need any new clothes.'

Krishnan tried to persuade Tim to change his mind, but he couldn't be persuaded. His T-shirt might have been old and a bit grubby, but he liked it.

'No problem,' said Krishnan. 'So, now you know my sister. She must escape from this place. You will help her?'

'I don't really understand why she needs our help,' said Tim, who was beginning to get a little impatient with Krishnan and all his crazy plans. 'We just walked in here. Why can't she just walk out?'

'Maybe this is possible,' said Krishnan. 'Maybe she could walk past the guards and walk out from the factory. Yes, it is indeed possible. But she will not go far. The blue rat will find her.'

'How?' said Tim. 'Can't you hide?'

'But it knows everything. Wherever you hide, it will find you.'

Natascha said, 'Can you tell me something, Krishnan? What's so special about this blue rat?'

'It is possessed of great powers,' said Krishnan. 'The blue rat is everywhere. It will find us and make terrible punishment. And not just us will be punished. It will send its men to our village. They will kill our mother and our father. They will take our brothers and our sisters and bring them back here. No, there is only one way to leave this factory. We must buy our freedom.'

Natascha looked up from her notebook. 'How are you going to do that?'

'I cannot,' said Krishnan. 'It is impossible for me to earn money. I can only sell books and the money is taken straight out of my hands. Maybe I beg some rupees from tourists on the train, but I need that money for food. For my sister, it is even more impossible. She cannot even leave the factory. She lives here always. She eats here, sleeps here, works here. That is why I have come to you,

Mister Tim. You must help me. You must give me money.'

'I don't have any money,' said Tim.

'This cannot be true,' said Krishnan. 'You are a rich man from a rich country. You are staying in a very nice hotel. I have seen the sheets and the soap in your room. These are not the sheets and the soap of a poor man. Mister Tim, I did not tell you this before, because I want you to see my sister with your own eyes. I want you to understand her situation. How bad it is. How much she needs your help. Now you have seen her. Do you understand? Will you help her? Will you save her from the blue rat?'

Tim didn't know what to say. He didn't know how to explain that, even if he had nice soap and smart sheets in his hotel room, he wasn't rich. His pocket money hardly paid for anything. If he wanted a new book or computer game, he had to wait till Christmas or his birthday. He couldn't think of any way to explain that without sounding stupid or spoilt, so he simply said, 'We don't have any money. We didn't bring any. We didn't know we'd need any. But if you take us back to the hotel, I'll talk to my dad and ask if I can borrow some from him.'

'Thank you, Mister Tim,' said Krishnan. He translated Tim's words to his sister. She grinned happily and raised her hands together in a *namaste*.

I don't know if I can help, Tim wanted to say. I'm just a boy. I don't have any savings. I've already spent this month's pocket money. I can ask Dad for a loan, but he'll probably say no.

Looking at Karishma's shining eyes and hopeful smile, Tim knew he couldn't say any of these things. Somehow, he would have to find a way to help her.

Natascha glanced at her watch. It was almost two o'clock. 'We have to go now,' she said. 'Otherwise we'll miss the tennis. I have to get to the courts in time to see my brother play his match.'

'Very good,' said Krishnan. He spoke a few words to his sister in Hindi, explaining what was happening. Karishma replied in Hindi. Krishnan angrily snapped back at her in the same language.

Tim said, 'What is she saying?'

'Oh, nothing, nothing.'

'She must be saying something.'

'She wants to come with us. But this is not a good time. She will come later, when you give me money.'

Karishma lifted her hands together and did a *namaste* to Tim and Natascha. They made the same gesture in return.

One of the girls peered through a hole in the wall which gave a clear view of the alleyway and watched the guards marching back and forth. When their backs were turned, she gestured to Krishnan. He sprinted out of the shack, followed by the others. They darted across the alleyway and, unseen by either of the guards, fled back the way that they had come.

Chapter 29

The four of them walked in a line: Krishnan first, then Natascha, with Tim and Grk following not far behind.

Grk sniffed the ground, searching for interesting scents, and Tim looked for good pictures to take.

Natascha kept glancing at her watch, calculating the time until Max's match started. She wanted to be sitting in her seat before he walked onto the court. She knew how much her presence mattered to her brother.

Krishnan moved fast, never pausing to listen for footsteps or voices. If he had been more cautious, he might have noticed who was following them.

Tim had taken a hundred and three photographs, but he wasn't satisfied yet. He wanted to take a perfect picture which would capture exactly what it felt like to be walking through the slum. Somehow, he wanted to find a way to capture the smells and the sounds as well as the sights of the slum. Maybe it was impossible. Maybe a photo just wasn't good enough. Maybe he'd have to come back with a movie camera instead. Nevertheless, he kept trying, snapping shots of the shacks, the mud, the rats and the children, trying to take the perfect photograph.

He was concentrating so hard on his camera that he didn't even notice when an arm shot out of the shadows and reached for him.

A hand grabbed Tim's wrist.

Tim shouted out, 'Wha—!'

Before he had a chance to speak another word, a second hand clamped over his mouth. Tim struggled so desperately that he dropped his camera on the ground, but he wasn't strong enough to free himself. The two arms held him in a tight grip.

Down on the ground, Grk whirled round and, without even pausing to think, jumped forward with his mouth open.

Whoever he was, Tim's captor must have been able to endure a lot of pain. When Grk's teeth clamped around his leg, he didn't scream or shout. He didn't even curse. He just swung his leg suddenly backwards, then forwards again.

Grk tried to hold on, but he wasn't strong enough. He had to let go. He flew through the air, landed on the other side of the alleyway, rolled over twice and sprang to his feet. Without even hesitating, he started barking loudly and furiously.

Krishnan and Natascha turned round to see what was wrong.

Tim couldn't see who was holding him so tightly, but he could see the shock and fear on Krishnan and Natascha's faces. And he could hear the voice which boomed from behind him. It was a deep voice, full of menace, and he had heard it somewhere before. 'Get that dog away from me! Get him away! Or I will break the neck of this boy!'

Natasha knew there was no point arguing. She ran forward, grabbed Grk's lead and pulled him away.

Tim felt himself being pushed from behind. His arms had been released. He stumbled forwards, taking two or three paces to regain his balance, then dodged down to the ground and grabbed his camera. When it was safely in his fist, he turned round and found himself facing a broad-shouldered man, wearing black trousers, black boots and a black shirt. Tim recognised him: he was the same guard who had seen them earlier and quizzed Krishnan about their presence in the factory.

Since then, the guard had discovered that there was no branch of the blue rat gang in London. He had realised that Krishnan had been lying. The two foreigners were intruders. He knew that now. And so he had come to find them.

The guard whistled. His two companions stepped out of the shadows. They raised their canes, ready to bring them crashing down on the children's heads.

There was no escape. Even with the assistance of an exceptionally brave and intelligent dog, the children could not get past three grown men armed with bamboo canes.

Speaking Hindi, Krishnan tried to argue with the guards, but they wouldn't be fooled a second time.

'Come!' said one of the guards. 'This way! The blue rat is waiting.'

Chapter 30

As the children hurried through the dark alleyways, the guards swished their bamboo canes through the air, warning Tim, Natascha and Krishnan what would happen if they made any attempt to escape.

When no one was watching, Tim slipped his camera into his pocket. If anyone confiscated his camera or deleted the photos, he would have no proof of what he had seen. He'd just have to hope that no one searched him.

Natascha glanced at her watch and shook her head. 'Max's match will start soon,' she said. 'We're going to miss the beginning.'

'How can you be worrying about matches at this moment?' said Krishnan. 'Do you not understand? This is no time for games!'

'Quiet!' snapped one of the guards, raising his fist. 'No talking!'

After that, none of the children uttered a single word. They didn't want to be punched with a fist or whipped with a bamboo cane.

They had been walking for a few minutes when they reached a shack which looked no different from the others. Four men stood outside, guarding the entrance, and eight more marched up and down the alleyway, watching anyone who came close.

One of the guards knocked three times on the shack's wooden door.

The door swung open.

The guards ushered the children into the shack.

From the outside, the shack looked like any of the other tumbledown huts in the slum. Its creaky walls were riddled with cracks. The roof looked as if it wouldn't provide any protection from a shower of rain and would be whisked away by a proper storm.

Inside, things weren't much different. The floor was damp and muddy. Scraps of straw poked down from the ceiling. A good shove with your shoulder would probably be enough to knock through one of these walls.

A small old woman was sitting cross-legged on the floor.

Tim stared at the old woman's face. She might have been sixty or eighty or even a hundred – he could never guess the age of adults – but her eyes retained the brightness and intelligence of youth. Her limbs were frail, her hair was white and her skin was scarred with wrinkles, but she still looked as if she had more energy and aggression than any of the strong, stern young men who surrounded her. She might not have been able to wrestle them or run faster than them, but she could still tell them exactly what to do and none of them would have dared to disobey her.

A small blue nose poked through the neckline of the old woman's white dress and twitched, sniffing the air.

The blue nose was followed by a blue body.

A blue rat crawled out of the old woman's dress and turned its head from side to side, sniffing and blinking.

The blue rat and the old woman lifted their heads and stared at the people who came into the room. Slowly, they inspected Tim, Natascha, Krishnan and Grk, letting their eyes wander over the three children and the dog.

The rat's whiskers twitched. It poked its nose into the old woman's ear.

The old woman appeared to listen to it for a few seconds. Then she smiled. When she spoke, her voice was soft and quiet. 'I know you,' she said, pointing at Krishnan. 'You are one of mine. Your name is Krishnan and you were born in Bihar. Yes?'

'Yes,' whispered Krishnan.

'But who are these two?' The old woman pointed at Tim and Natascha.

'My name is Tim,' said Tim. 'And this is Grk.' He pointed at Grk.

'And I'm Natascha Raffifi,' said Natascha.

The blue rat sniffed and blinked. Its whiskers twitched. It poked its nose into the old woman's ear and appeared to whisper again.

The old woman said, 'Tell me, Tim and Grk and Natascha Raffifi, what are you doing here?'

'We've come to help Krishnan,' said Tim.

'This boy doesn't need your help,' said the old woman. 'He can look after himself. He works every day, making good money. He doesn't need anything from any foreigners.'

Tim said, 'And what happens to all that money?'

'It goes to the blue rat,' said the old woman.

'You mean, it goes to you.'

'No. Not me. The blue rat takes everything.'

Tim shook his head. 'That's just ridiculous,' he said. 'Rats don't need money. You're just using the rat to get money for yourself. You've got hundreds of children working for you. I've seen them. On the trains. In the streets. All of them are making money – and you get to keep all of it!'

The old woman shook her head. 'You don't understand anything,' she said. 'You're just a stupid foreigner.'

'I understand everything!' said Tim. 'You're using the blue rat to cheat people and—'

'Enough!' The old woman's voice cut through the air, interrupting Tim and stopping him from saying another word. She gestured at the guards. They stepped forward.

Tim knew that if he continued speaking, the guards would hit him. So he kept quiet.

In the silence, the old woman turned her head slightly, angling her face towards the blue rat, listening to it.

The rat's tail curled and uncurled as if it had a life of its own. It lifted its head and poked its nose into the old woman's ear.

The old woman appeared to listen to it for a few seconds. Then she smiled. 'The blue rat has spoken,' she said. 'He says you must die.' She nodded at the guards. 'Take them to the pit.'

As soon as the old woman said these words, Krishnan took two quick steps towards her.

The guards tensed, reaching for their weapons, thinking that Krishnan was going to attack their leader, but he just threw himself down on the floor at her feet. His arms outstretched, he begged for mercy. 'Please,' moaned Krishnan in a pitiful tone. 'Please, take me. Please, kill me. But not them. They have done nothing to you. Let them go back to their own country.'

The old woman wasn't interested. Nor was the blue rat. Neither of them even looked at Krishnan. The old woman just gestured to the waiting guards, ordering them to take the children away, then turned her back on them.

Cupping her hands, she lifted the blue rat from her shoulder and placed him gently on the floor.

The blue rat scurried towards a shallow earthenware bowl which was filled with fresh milk. Placing both front paws on the rim, it lifted itself over the edge, dipped its head into the bowl and started drinking.

It hadn't taken more than three sips when its meal was rudely interrupted. Grk ran across the floor and grabbed the blue rat by the scruff of its neck.

For a moment, no one moved. They were all too shocked.

The blue rat was sacred. It was like a god. People did whatever it said. But this dog had just picked it up in his teeth! What did he think he was doing? Didn't he understand the power of the blue rat?

The old woman was the first to recover from her shock. She screamed. 'Stop him! Stop him!'

The guards yelled. 'Drop that rat! Drop it!'

Some of them drew their guns, but they couldn't shoot. They might have shot the rat rather than the dog. And they all knew what would happen to them if they made the mistake of killing the blue rat.

Grk took no notice of what anyone screamed or yelled. He didn't care about the old woman or the guards. He just held the rat in his mouth and looked at Tim as if to say: 'What shall we do now?'

Chapter 31

Just like the other children who lived in the slum, Krishnan never went to school. He couldn't read or write. He didn't know any history or geography. Maths was a mystery to him.

But he knew other things instead. How to survive, for instance. How to steal. How to beg. How to follow someone without being heard. How to pick a man's pockets and steal his wallet without him noticing. Where to sleep if you find yourself alone in the city at night. Where to scavenge some scraps of food if your belly is empty and you don't have any money. And all kinds of other skills which, perhaps, might be more useful than reading, writing, history, geography and maths.

They would certainly have helped Tim.

If you had given Tim a map of the world, he could have pointed out Paris, Moscow, Sydney and Los Angeles. If you'd ask him to multiply eight by seven, he wouldn't have paused to think before he said fifty-six. He could have told you when William the Conqueror landed at Hastings and the dates of the First World War. But he had absolutely no idea how to escape from a room full of armed men.

Luckily, he got some help.

Krishnan bounded forward, reached into the holster of one of the guards who was standing nearby and grabbed his gun. He pointed the gun at the old woman and said, 'Let us go. Or you die.'

The old woman cursed him in Hindi.

Krishnan took no notice. He just repeated what he had said before. 'Let us go. Or you die.'

The old woman said, 'What about the blue rat?'

'You can have him. If you let us go.'

The old woman thought for a moment, then agreed. She didn't really have any choice.

Krishnan told her exactly what to do.

The old woman walked to the door and addressed the guards who were standing outside. She told all of them to drop their weapons on the ground and allow the children to walk past. The guards could hardly believe their ears, but they did exactly what they were told. They put their guns down and stood aside, leaving a clear path from the door of the hut to the end of the alleyway.

Krishnan, Tim and Natascha emerged from the hut and walked to the end of the alleyway. Grk walked with them, the blue rat dangling from his mouth.

None of the guards followed them. The old woman had ordered them not to and they always did whatever she said. But even if they hadn't been ordered to stand still, they would have done. They were rooted to the spot with shock. All of them had believed that the blue rat was a god. All of them had trusted in the blue rat's power. And now – what were they supposed to think? The blue rat was dangling from the mouth of a little dog.

If the blue rat was a god, shouldn't he be able to save himself?

If the blue rat had great powers, why didn't he jump out of the dog's mouth?

What was wrong with the blue rat?

Krishnan kept the gun fixed on the old woman until the last possible moment. When they reached the end of the alleyway, he nodded to the others. 'Let's go,' he said.

Tim said, 'Drop the rat!'

Natascha said, 'Go on! Drop it!'

Grk opened his mouth and dropped the rat on the ground. At exactly the same moment, Krishnan threw the gun into the shadows.

And then the four of them sprinted round the corner and ran as fast as they could.

While the children ran in one direction, the blue rat ran in the other. It sped along the alleyway and leaped into the old woman's arms.

For a moment, the old woman did nothing except hug her blue rat. She kissed his little pointed nose and stroked his long springy whiskers. When she was convinced that the blue rat hadn't been harmed, she turned to her guards.

'Find those children,' she said, 'and when you have found them, kill them.'

Chapter 32

They ran.

Krishnan led the way. Tim and Natascha came next. Grk followed close behind. For once in his life, Grk never stopped to have a pee. He never even paused to sniff some interesting smells. He just ran.

Behind them, they could hear the sound of piercing whistles. That was the guards. They were summoning reinforcements.

'This way!' yelled Krishnan. He ducked down an alleyway and, without waiting to see if the others had followed him, started running as fast as his skinny little legs would carry him.

Natascha, Tim and Grk sprinted after him.

Behind them, they heard pounding footsteps. The guards weren't far behind. And they were coming closer.

Krishnan never hesitated. He knew exactly where he was going. Dodging left, then right, then left, then right again, he led them down alleyway after alleyway, leaping over drains and puddles, ducking through gateways and under overhanging roofs, and finally emerging into a crowded street.

'Here!' he shouted breathlessly to the others. 'In here!'

He threw himself into an empty auto-rickshaw which had been parked by the side of the road.

*

At a café on the other side of the street, a man named Hari Karamchand pushed back his chair and shouted, 'Hello? Hello? Can I help you?'

Every day, whatever the weather, Hari drove around the streets of Delhi in his auto-rickshaw, picking up passengers. Like most of the auto-rickshaws on the streets of Delhi, this three-wheel taxi was painted black, green and yellow. It had a windscreen but no windows on the sides.

On a good day, Hari made a few hundred rupees, enough to pay his rent and feed his family. On a bad day, he drove home empty-handed and his children went to bed hungry.

When Hari saw three children and a dog clambering into his auto-rickshaw, he assumed that they wanted a lift. After all, what else could they possibly be doing? Why would you clamber inside an auto-rickshaw if you didn't want a lift?

Tossing a couple of coins on the table to pay for his cup of *chai*, Hari started strolling back to his auto-rickshaw.

'Hello!' he shouted again. 'Hello! Hello! Where do you want to go? Connaught Place? New Delhi Station? Wherever you are headed, I will give you a good price!'

The children heard what Hari Karamchand was saying, but they ignored him. Not because they were rude. They just had too many other things to think about.

Krishnan ushered Natascha into the back of the auto-rickshaw. Grk sprang after her. Tim sat alongside Krishnan on the front seat.

Krishnan started the engine.

Glancing in the mirrors to his left and right, Tim saw the first guards emerging from the same alleyway that they had just left. 'Hurry,' he said. 'They've found us.'

'Then let's go,' replied Krishnan. 'Go! Go! Go!'

'Go where?' said Tim. 'And do what?'

'Just grab them and steer.'

Following Krishnan's instructions, Tim grabbed the handlebars. (Like a bike, auto-rickshaws have handlebars rather than a steering wheel.) Krishnan thrust his hand down onto the accelerator.

The auto-rickshaw sped forwards.

For a moment, Hari was too surprised to do anything. He couldn't move. He couldn't even speak. Those three children – and that dog – didn't want a lift in his beloved auto-rickshaw. They wanted to steal it!

'Thief!' he shouted. 'Stop, thief!'

But the children showed no sign of stopping. If anything, they sped up.

Hari sprinted across the street in pursuit, waving his arms and shouting. 'Come here! Come back here! You dirty little thieves, bring that back here!'

Auto-rickshaws are designed to be driven by adults, not children. A child can't reach the handlebars and the accelerator pedal at the same time. That's why Tim and Krishnan had to drive it together, one of them steering and the other controlling the accelerator. Krishnan crouched on the floor, both hands pressed down on the accelerator, while Tim gripped the handlebars and steered the auto-rickshaw down the street.

Tim had never driven an auto-rickshaw before. With any luck, he would never have to drive one again. He was a terrible driver.

Veering wildly from one side of the road to the other, he steered the auto-rickshaw through the traffic, skidding round a bus and weaving through a line of cars.

Brakes screeched. Drivers yelled. Pedestrians jumped for their lives. It was a miracle that no one got killed.

The auto-rickshaw clipped a market stall. Melons and mangoes bounced along the road. The stallholder lost his balance. His purse went flying. Children scrabbled for coins.

Two cars swerved to avoid Tim's auto-rickshaw. They slammed together. Metal crunched and glass tinkled. The drivers jumped out and started yelling at one another, each blaming the other.

Tim heard the crash and the shouting, and knew it had been his fault, but didn't stop to say sorry. All his attention was concentrated on the road ahead. As Krishnan pressed down harder on the accelerator and the engine whirred faster, Tim steered round buses and trucks, bikes and cows, dogs and people, goats and chickens, trying to put as much distance as possible between him and his pursuers.

Guards were pouring out of the slum.

Two guards leaped into a taxi. When the driver protested, they put a gun to his head. Without another word, the driver jumped out of the door and ran, leaving the guards to take his car.

Other guards grabbed bicycles, auto-rickshaws, cycle-rickshaws and scooters. They jumped into the saddles, put their feet on the pedals or kick-started the engines, and lifted their heads, searching for any sign of the children, trying to decide which way to go.

The busy street didn't look very different from any other busy street in Delhi. It was packed with cars, trucks, buses, bicycles, cows, dogs, goats, chickens, people and auto-rickshaws.

Hundreds of auto-rickshaws. Thousands of auto-rickshaws. Millions of auto-rickshaws. The city was full of auto-rickshaws. And every single one looked exactly the same.

The guards sat on their bicycles, auto-rickshaws, cycle-rickshaws and scooters, not knowing what to do or which way to go.

Chapter 33

Max swung his racket hopelessly and missed the ball.

'Love-forty,' said the umpire.

Max shook his head. He couldn't understand what was wrong with him. This was the worst game of tennis that he'd ever played in his entire life. He crossed to the other half of the court and prepared to serve.

The game had lasted little more than an hour and Mustafa Myrtle had won almost every point. He had taken the first set six-love. Now, he was leading four-love in the second set. If he won one more point and then one more game, Mustafa Myrtle would win the match.

Once more, Max told himself to stop thinking about his sister.

Of course he was worried about her disappearance. Of course he was concerned that she and Tim and Grk were nowhere to be seen. But none of that mattered. For now, he just needed to concentrate on this game of tennis. He could worry about Natascha later.

He bounced the ball on the ground and served. Once again, his arm seemed to lack any strength, his eyes hardly focused and his mind was elsewhere.

With a confident swing of his racket, Mustafa Myrtle whacked the ball back about ten times harder, speeding it across the court, putting it beyond Max's reach.

'Game, Myrtle,' said the umpire. 'Myrtle leads by five games to love and by one set to love.'

Mustafa Myrtle jogged confidently to his chair, grabbed a drink and towel, and sat down, determined to make maximum use of the one minute break.

Max walked slowly and dejectedly to his chair. When he sat down, he glanced across the court at the place where his sister should have been sitting. But she wasn't there. He could see four empty seats in a row. One for Tim, one for Natascha and two for the Malts.

Mr and Mrs Malt couldn't come to the game. They were searching for Tim, Natascha and Grk.

The two children had promised that they wouldn't leave the hotel, but they had disappeared. No one knew where they had gone. No one had even seen them since nine o'clock that morning. Now, the Malts and every available member of the hotel's staff were searching for them, checking the rooms, the cupboards, the gym, the restaurants, the terraces and every other part of the hotel, searching for a boy, a girl and a dog.

Max dropped his head and stared at his shoes.

I have to forget about Natascha, Max told himself. I have to stop worrying about her. I have to concentrate on my game.

But he couldn't.

While Natascha was missing, he couldn't think about tennis. All his attention was focused on his sister, wondering what had happened to her and worrying where she might be.

'Time,' called the umpire, announcing the end of the break and the beginning of the next game.

The crowd cheered and applauded, shouting encouragement to the players.

Mustafa Myrtle jogged to his place and nodded to the ball boy.

Max Raffifi took a little more time, wiping his face with a damp towel, swallowing a gulp of water and strolling slowly to his place.

If he lost this game, he would lose the whole match. But that didn't matter. He would be able to go back to the hotel and join the search for his sister. He might have tried to convince himself otherwise, but he knew what he really thought. Finding Natascha was much more important than winning a game of tennis.

Mustafa Myrtle bounced a ball on the ground and prepared to serve.

There was a commotion at the far side of the court. Some people were trying to take their seats, but the guards wouldn't let them inside until the game had finished.

Mustafa Myrtle waited, holding the ball in one hand and his racket in the other, not wanting to serve until the disturbance had finished.

The umpire leaned forward and spoke clearly into his microphone. 'Quiet, please. Could we have silence in the court, please. Thank you. Mustafa Myrtle to serve.'

Despite the umpire's intervention, the noise seemed to get even louder. The two newcomers refused to be dissuaded. Before Mustafa had had a chance to serve, a boy and a girl burst past the guards.

Tim and Natascha hurried across the court to their seats.

Dogs weren't allowed inside the tennis club, so they had left Grk by the gates with Krishnan.

When Tim and Natascha had sat down, the umpire called for silence once more. 'Quiet, please. Thank you. Mustafa Myrtle to serve.'

As Mustafa Myrtle bounced the ball on the ground, preparing to serve, Max Raffifi lifted his head and glanced at Natascha.

Max and Natascha didn't speak. Their expressions hardly changed. But a kind of signal passed between them.

Mustafa Myrtle hit the ball, firing a fast serve across the court. Max took two quick steps and whacked the ball back again, positioning it precisely where Mustafa couldn't reach it.

'Love-fifteen,' said the umpire.

From that moment onwards, Max won every point.

Chapter 34

In the first break of play, Tim borrowed a phone from the people in the next seat and rang his parents. He explained that he and Natascha were sitting safely in the New Delhi Lawn Tennis Club, watching Max play Mustafa Myrtle.

Mr and Mrs Malt immediately caught a taxi from the hotel and came to the tennis club. When they arrived, they didn't scold Tim or Natascha. That could wait till later. For now, they were so relieved to see the two children, they didn't do anything except hug them.

The four of them sat in a row and watched Max defeat Mustafa Myrtle.

After the match, the Malts, Natascha and Grk went onto the court and congratulated Max.

He hugged everyone in turn. First Natascha, then Tim, then Grk, then Mr Malt, then Mrs Malt and finally Natascha again.

Max was feeling triumphant. He was through to the third round of the championship. Tomorrow, he would play an American boy named Tommy Barnard. If he won that match, he would get to play in the quarter-finals. If he won that and the semi-final, he would be in the final. He might even win the whole competition.

Vijay Ghat strolled across the court, accompanied by his advisers, and came to shake hands with Max. Photographers crowded round and took pictures. Tomorrow morning, these photographs would be seen all around India, plastered over the pages of every Indian newspaper.

'Congratulations,' said Vijay Ghat. 'That was a magnificent victory. I wish you every success in your next game.'

'Thank you,' said Max.

Vijay Ghat smiled at Tim and Natascha. 'You must be very proud of him.'

For a moment, neither Tim nor Natascha replied. And then Tim said, 'Why don't you stop the blue rat gang?'

'Excuse me?' said Vijay Ghat.

Tim repeated the question. 'Why don't you stop the blue rat gang?'

'I have no idea what you're talking about,' said Vijay Ghat. 'Who or what is the blue rat gang?'

'We'll show you,' said Tim. 'Look.'

He pulled out his camera and went through some of the shots that he had taken in the slums, allowing Vijay Ghat to see them on the screen. At the same time, Natascha opened her notebook and read some of the notes that she had taken, describing comments or conversations or particular scenes that she had witnessed.

Vijay Ghat looked and listened in silence.

Journalists and photographers gathered round, taking notes and pictures, recording exactly what was happening. Tomorrow morning, newspapers all around

India would carry descriptions of this moment. Everyone in the country would know the name of the blue rat gang – and everyone would know that Vijay Ghat did too.

When Tim and Natascha had finished their description of the blue rat gang, Vijay Ghat glanced at the crowd of journalists, then spoke to the children in a calm, kind voice, making sure that everyone could hear exactly what he was saying. 'I am shocked by what you've just shown me,' he said. 'Children should never have to work like this. These children have been robbed of their childhood by the blue rat gang. This is a terrible, terrible thing.'

'We know,' said Tim.

'That's why we've shown you these pictures,' said Natascha.

'But there is one thing that I don't understand,' said Vijay Ghat. 'Why are you showing this to *me*? What is the connection between these terrible criminals and *me*?'

'You're one of the richest men in India,' said Tim. 'Aren't you?'

'Well, yes, I suppose I am.'

'Which means you could have whatever you want. Couldn't you?'

'I suppose that's true,' said Vijay Ghat.

'It is true,' said Natascha.

'And this is how you've chosen to spend your money,' said Tim. He spread his arms, encompassing the tennis court, the umpire, the players and the people who had come to watch the game.

Vijay Ghat nodded. It was indisputably true that he had chosen to spend some of his millions on the Vijay Ghat International Lawn Tennis Association Under-Sixteen Championship.

'You've paid for this whole tennis tournament,' said Tim. 'You've flown players from all around the world to be here. And that's great. But don't you think you should give some of your money to your own country too? Don't you think you should do something to help all the children who have been attacked and abused by the blue rat gang? You've got more money than you know what to do with. Why don't you spend some of it on helping other people?'

For a few moments, Vijay Ghat stood in silence and said nothing. He thought about what Tim had just said. He looked at the crowd of journalists who were watching and recording the conversations. Then he turned to Tim and Natascha and spoke in a slow, serious voice.

'I want to thank you,' said Vijay Ghat. 'Both of you. I want to thank you very much. You have exposed something terrible at the heart of this city and this country. With your help, we are going to change it. Come on, children. Come with me. We are going to do exactly what you suggest. From today, the blue rat gang will never have the chance to hurt another child.'

Perhaps Vijay Ghat really did care about all the children who had been stolen by the blue rat gang and were now working in the slums. Or perhaps he simply didn't want any bad publicity associated with his name and his tennis tournament. For whatever reason, he summoned his advisers and demanded immediate action.

One of Vijay Ghat's men rang the Chief of Police and insisted that the blue rat gang had to be arrested. Vijay Ghat wanted the blue rat gang to be broken up, he explained, and he wanted all the children in the blue rat gang's factory to be freed.

If you or I rang the Chief of Police and asked him to do something, he probably wouldn't take any notice of us. He might tell us to call back tomorrow or talk to his secretary. But you and I aren't as rich or powerful as Vijay Ghat.

Later that day, several hundred police surrounded the factory. They searched every hut. Thousands of CDs, DVDs, books and clothes were seized. All the children working for the blue rat gang were freed from their slavery. The police arranged for them to be sent home to their villages and reunited with their parents.

Each of the children returned home with a present from Vijay Ghat: a payment of ten thousand rupees to help them and their families.

There was only one problem. Not a single arrest was made.

When the police arrived, the slum was packed with children, but there weren't any adults to be seen. Somehow, the old woman and their gang must have known that the police were coming. All of them had vanished.

It was the blue rat, some people said. The blue rat knew the police were coming. He had warned his gang to run away. With his help, the entire gang had managed to escape.

Other people said that the blue rat was just a fake. A dog had picked the blue rat up in his mouth, they said. If a dog could do that, the blue rat must have lost its power. That was why the gang had disbanded and disappeared.

Yet more people said that the blue rat had never had any power in the first place. It was just an ordinary rat which had been painted blue. An evil woman had used it to scare superstitious villagers into giving away their children.

No one knew who or what to believe.

All around Delhi, people were talking about the blue rat. All of them had different theories. And all of them were asking the same questions.

'Where is the blue rat now? And what is he going to do next?'

Chapter 35

It was the final day of the Vijay Ghat International Lawn Tennis Association Under-Sixteen Championship. Only one match was left to be played. Whoever won this match would win the tournament.

The two finalists were named Vilayati Jeera and Max Raffifi.

A large crowd had gathered to watch. The court was packed with people.

And not just people.

In the long and distinguished history of the New Delhi Lawn Tennis Club, not a single dog had ever been permitted to pass between the two tall iron gates.

Until today.

In the morning, the officials of the New Delhi Lawn Tennis Club received a phone call from Vijay Ghat. He had a special request. The officials immediately agreed to make an exception to their usual rules.

Accompanied by Tim, Natascha, the Malts, and Krishnan and Karishma, Grk had been given a seat in the President's Box to watch the final of the Vijay Ghat International Lawn Tennis Association Under-Sixteen Championship.

'Silence, please,' said the umpire. 'Max Raffifi to serve.'

The crowd went quiet.

Tim and Natascha leaned forward in their seats, staring at the court. Both of them were almost too nervous to breathe.

Max bounced the ball several times on the ground. He looked cool, calm and confident. But he wasn't. If you had known him as well as Natascha and Tim did, you would have been able to tell that he was actually exceedingly nervous.

Max threw the ball in the air, swung his racket and served.

The game had begun.

The two opponents were evenly matched. Each of them served brilliantly. Max won the first game. Vilayati Jeera won the second. Max won the third. Vilayati Jeera won the fourth. Now, Max was serving in the fifth.

Between each point, people cheered and whistled, but no one made a noise while the ball was whizzing back and forth across the court. The whole crowd was rigid with tension.

Except Grk.

He was whining, pawing the floor and restlessly swivelling his head from side to side. He kept wrinkling his nostrils and sniffing the air as if he could smell something horrible.

He might have been bored or cross or restless or desperate for a pee. Or he could have been trying to communicate something to the others. Whatever he was doing, his efforts weren't working. No one took any notice of him.

It's always frustrating when people don't understand what you're trying to say. But Grk wasn't just frustrated. He was desperate.

He nudged Tim's leg with his muzzle, but Tim pushed him away, wanting to concentrate on the game.

Grk turned to Natascha and pushed his head against her shins, trying to attract her attention.

'Not now,' whispered Natascha. 'I'm busy.' She leaned forward, her chin resting on her hands, and stared at the court, willing Max to win this point.

Grk had tried his best to attract their attention politely, but he had failed. Now, he was left with no other choice. He'd have to be rude. He opened his mouth and barked.

Woof woof!

The noise echoed up and down the court. Thousands of people turned to stare. Thousands more whispered to one another, wondering where that noise had come from. Was there a dog in here? Weren't animals banned from the tennis club? Can you see it? Oh, yes! Look! Over there! That little white dog! How did he get in here?

Mrs Malt stared at Tim and Natascha with tight lips. 'Keep that animal under control,' she hissed. 'Or he'll have to go outside. Do you understand?'

Tim nodded. 'Yes, Mum.'

'Shhh,' said Natascha to Grk. 'Shhh! No noise while the game's going on.'

Grk looked up at her with sad eyes. He knew he was behaving badly, but he couldn't help himself. He had no

164

choice. He opened his mouth and barked again, even louder.

Woof woof!

Natascha wagged her finger. 'Bad boy! Bad boy! No barking!'

The umpire leaned forward and spoke into his microphone. 'Quiet, please! Quiet! Could you please be quiet!'

As if he was replying to the umpire, Grk barked again.

Woof woof!

Natascha leaned down, grabbed Grk, pulled him onto her lap and clamped her hands around his muzzle, preventing him from opening his mouth.

'Thank you,' said the umpire, once he was satisfied that the barking had stopped. 'Max Raffifi to serve.'

Max bounced the ball on the ground three times, then drew his racket behind his head and threw the ball high into the air.

On Natascha's lap, Grk whined and wriggled, desperately trying to free himself.

Chapter 36

Tim didn't understand what was happening. He'd never seen Grk like this before. Grk might have been mischievous, and was even occasionally cunning, but he was never normally naughty. When he was told to keep quiet, he never usually made a sound.

Maybe he was desperate for a pee. Maybe he'd found a chilli on the ground and chomped it down, not realising how its heat would upset his stomach. Or maybe he just hated tennis.

Tim knew that he couldn't expect Natascha to take Grk out of the court. She was absorbed by the game, hardly breathing during the points, cheering at the top of her voice when Max won a point and flopping back in her seat when he lost.

There was another reason why Natascha needed to stay in her seat. Every few moments, Max glanced across the court and looked at her, taking strength from her presence. If Natascha took Grk outside, perhaps Max wouldn't be able to play so well. He might start losing every point, just as he had done in the match against Mustafa Myrtle.

At the end of the next game, when the two players had a minute's break before changing ends, Tim stood up.

'I'll take Grk for a pee,' he said. 'I think he's desperate.'

Natascha half-heartedly offered to accompany Tim too, but showed no real enthusiasm for leaving her seat. She really wanted to stay and watch the rest of the game.

'Don't worry,' said Tim. 'I'll be fine. I won't go further than the entrance of the court and then I'll come straight back again.'

Mr and Mrs Malt glanced at one another. Neither of them liked letting Tim venture out of the court alone, but they trusted him not to do anything stupid.

'Come back quickly,' said Mr Malt.

'If you're not back in one minute,' said Mrs Malt, 'we'll come and find you.'

'Don't worry,' said Tim. 'I'll be quick.'

He stood up and tugged Grk's lead. The dog leaped happily to his feet, delighted to be leaving the court. Perhaps he really was desperate for a pee. Or perhaps he just hated tennis.

Together, the boy and the dog walked down the line of chairs. As they pushed past other spectators, Tim apologised to them and Grk sniffed their shoes.

Just as they reached the exit, there was a roar from the crowd. People cheered and applauded. The break had ended. The players were returning to the court.

'Let's be quick,' Tim whispered to Grk. 'I don't want to miss more than one game.'

Together, the boy and the dog walked out of the court and emerged at the base of the stands. Above them, thousands of people were crammed into the seats. Tim wondered where he might find a piece of grass or some dirty concrete where Grk could have a pee, but he'd hardly had time to cast his eyes around when his right hand was pulled with a great wrench. Grk was already hurrying down a shadowy alleyway, pulling Tim behind him on the taut lead.

Tim whispered, 'Where are you going?'

Grk took no notice. Tugging the lead, he headed into the shadows.

'What's the hurry?' whispered Tim.

But Grk just carried on tugging the lead, trying to pull Tim down the alleyway that led under the stands.

Oh, well, thought Tim. Grk probably knows the perfect place to pee. Not knowing where they were going or why, and not really caring, Tim followed Grk into the shadows.

Grk trotted left, then right, then left again, confidently negotiating the dark spaces under the stands.

Every few moments, noises echoed around them from the crowds crammed into the seats above them: shuffling feet, clapping hands, a roar of triumph or a sigh of despair.

Tim thought about all the people sitting above him. It was a creepy feeling. If the metal struts warped or broke, several thousand of them would fall straight down on top of him.

They had been walking for a minute or two when Grk stopped and turned round, his tail wagging slowly from side to side. He looked up at Tim, waiting for his reaction.

At first, Tim couldn't see clearly into the darkness. He could distinguish nothing more than a few shadowy forms and what looked like a small bright red light. Then his eyes adjusted to the gloom and he realised he was looking at a bomb.

Chapter 37

The old woman breathed slowly and carefully.

The blue rat was squatting on her shoulder, but she took no notice of him. All her attention was concentrated on the bomb, the timer and the detonator.

Behind her, the four men waited and watched. No one spoke. No one even moved.

All of them understood that the bomb was an unstable creation. If it was mishandled or even given an accidental nudge, it might detonate.

If that happened, they wouldn't have a moment to take a breath or say a word before the explosion obliterated them. And not just them. It would destroy the people sitting in the rows of seats above them and most of the New Delhi Lawn Tennis Club too.

The bright red display read 15:00.

The old woman stretched her arm forward and clicked a switch, activating the bomb and starting the timer.

Now the display read 14:59.

The countdown had begun. Fourteen minutes and fifty-nine seconds from now, the timer would reach zero and the bomb would blow up.

The old woman turned her back on the bomb and looked at each of her companions in turn.

No one spoke. There was nothing to say. Each of them knew exactly what the others were thinking.

The display read 14.53.

Fourteen minutes and fifty-three seconds from now, a massive ball of fire would roar in every direction, devastating everything in its path. The tennis club would be destroyed. The stands would collapse. Thousands of people would die.

The old woman's lips lifted in a smile. With one blow, she would take revenge on several of her enemies. Those children. That dog. And Vijay Ghat. All of them had believed that they could break up the blue rat gang. They had made her look like a fool in front of the whole world. Well, she would show them. She would destroy Vijay Ghat as punishment for closing her factory. She would kill those two foreigners, the boy and the girl, who had caused the blue rat gang so much trouble. And, by destroying them with such swiftness and brutality, she would demonstrate exactly what happens to anyone who challenged the blue rat.

The old woman nodded to the four men. 'Let's go,' she said.

Relief flooded their faces. Glancing at the timer, which now read 14.48, they knew the bomb would go off in precisely fourteen minutes and forty-eight seconds. Between now and then, they wanted to put as much distance as possible between the tennis club and themselves. They didn't want to be anywhere near this bomb when it blew up. All of them picked up their

171

tools and turned to go.

That was when the blue rat saw Grk.

Issuing a shrill cry of alarm, the blue rat darted down the old woman's dress and sprang to the floor.

The old woman turned her head. She saw Tim and Grk standing in the shadows. She didn't waste time asking questions or wondering how they might have found her. She just hissed furiously, issuing a quick order to her men.

The four guards whirled round, reaching for their pistols. But before they had a chance to draw their guns, Grk charged at the blue rat.

At that moment, several things happened at once. A roar of cheering and applause came from the seats above them. The old woman shouted another order. The blue rat turned and ran. Grk sprinted after him.

The guards didn't know what to do. Should they shoot Tim? Chase the dog? Grab the rat? Or get out of here before the bomb blew up? They looked at the old woman for guidance.

'Kill the boy,' she said.

Four pistols lifted and pointed. Four fingers tightened on four triggers. Four bullets slammed into the spot where Tim had just been standing.

'Get him!' screeched the old woman. 'Get him!'

The four guards ran after Tim. The old woman ran in the opposite direction. She had only one thought in her mind: she wanted the rat back. With one bite, a dog could break the rat's neck. She wasn't going to let

172

that happen. Darting after Grk, the old woman plunged into the darkness, all other worries forgotten.

The timer blinked. In fourteen minutes and thirty-three seconds, the bomb would explode.

Chapter 38

Tim ran as fast he could, dodging through the darkness, but he didn't have a clue where he was going.

Grk had led him to the old woman, the blue rat and their bomb. Alone, unaided by Grk's sense of smell, Tim couldn't find his own way out. He had no idea which way to go.

But he didn't have time to worry about getting out of here. That wasn't important. He just needed to stay alive.

Any second now, a bullet might whizz through the air, puncture the skin between his shoulder blades and smash into his spine, hurling him to the floor.

He turned left, then right, then left again, pushing through the gloom, hoping he wouldn't smack into some hidden obstacle that was impossible to see in this darkness.

Ahead of him, he could see something. A white shape. Down on the ground.

What was it? Could it be . . . ?

Yes. It was.

Grk wagged his tail as if to say: 'What took you so long? I've been waiting here for ages.'

There was no sign of the blue rat. Maybe Grk had already caught him and killed him. Or maybe Grk had been eluded by him. Or Grk might even have decided that looking after Tim was more important than breaking the neck of some little rat. For whatever reason, Grk was here now, his tail wagging, his tongue half-hanging out of the mouth.

Tim said, 'Do you know how to get out of here?'

Grk's tail wagged even faster. He turned and ran down the corridor, then paused, his head turned, waiting for Tim to follow him.

'I hope you're right,' said Tim.

He ran after Grk.

Behind him, he could hear the sound of footsteps and heavy breathing and four men shouting to one another. He took no notice. There was no point worrying about them. He just ran as fast as he could, following Grk through the gloom.

Chapter 39

The score was six games all.

The first set would be decided by a tie-break. Max Raffifi and Vilayati Jeera faced one another across the net. Both of them were desperately trying to hide their nerves.

The crowd was quiet. No one moved. No one spoke.

Vilayati Jeera bounced the ball on the ground. He bounced it again. Then he threw it into the air, swung his racket and delivered one of his fastest serves. The ball whistled across the court at a hundred and three miles an hour.

Max was ready. He whacked the ball back again, skilfully sending it to Vilayati Jeera's backhand.

The ball slammed back and forth across the court. The two players were perfectly matched. Backhand and forehand, lob and smash, they tried all their tricks but neither of them could outwit the other. The rally looked as if it could have gone on forever.

And maybe it would have done if two intruders hadn't pushed past the guards and run onto the court.

Distracted by the extraordinary sight of a boy and a dog running onto the court, Max completely bungled his return, hitting the ball straight up into the air. It landed in the middle of the crowd.

But no one noticed. Not even the umpire. They were all staring in astonishment at the unexpected intruders.

No one could believe what was happening.

No one said a word or made a sound.

The guards, ball boys, spectators, umpire and players had all been reduced to stunned silence.

All except one.

'Oh, Tim,' whispered Mrs Malt. 'What are you doing?'

If Tim heard her, he didn't show it. Nor did Grk. The two of them just ran over to the chair where the umpire was sitting.

At the entrance to the court, the old woman's four guards stared at one another. They couldn't go any further. Not without being caught. And if they were caught, they would be held here and forced to answer all kinds of questions.

They didn't care about the questions. They cared about being forced to remain here. Nothing could be worse than still being here ten minutes from now, when a huge explosion would rip the whole place to pieces.

The old woman would have to look after herself. So would her rat. The four men just wanted to save themselves. Pocketing their pistols, they turned and ran towards the exit.

The umpire's name was Naga Caraway Singh. He was fifty-five years old. Long ago, he had played at Wimbledon. He had been knocked out in the first round, but he hadn't minded. As far as Naga Caraway Singh was concerned, playing was more important than winning.

For the past twelve years, Naga Caraway Singh had worked as an umpire at the New Delhi Lawn Tennis Club. During that time, he had officiated at almost five hundred games of tennis. He had witnessed walkovers and comebacks, tantrums and fist fights, black eyes and broken wrists, sprained ankles and cut lips. He had heard men and women curse in fifty different languages. Once, he had even watched one player smash his racket over the head of another. He thought he'd seen everything.

But he had never seen a boy and a dog run across a tennis court in the middle of a match, dodging the outstretched arms of guards and ball boys, and charge straight towards the umpire's chair.

Naga Caraway Singh leaned forward. Trying to stay very calm, he spoke slowly and clearly into his microphone. 'Young man,' he said, 'what on earth do you think you are doing?'

Without answering, Tim grabbed the microphone.

Naga Caraway Singh blinked twice and opened his mouth, but was so surprised that he couldn't say a single word.

Tim didn't mind. He had something to say. And he didn't want to be interrupted. Turning to face the crowd, he raised the microphone to his lips.

Usually, this microphone was used for announcing who had won each point and what the score was. Tim had a much more important announcement to make.

'There is a bomb under this tennis court,' he said. 'It's going to go off in five minutes. You have to get out of here.'

Some of the spectators laughed, assuming he must be joking. A few more took photos, thinking this must be some kind of prank. Maybe they were on a TV show. Soon, they would probably see a famous TV presenter sauntering onto the court to announce that they had all been filmed and telling them when the show was going to broadcast.

Photographers swivelled their cameras to record the scene. Tomorrow morning, every newspaper in India would carry a picture of this crazy boy and his little dog, explaining how they had disrupted the final of the Vijay Ghat International Lawn Tennis Association Under-Sixteen Championship.

Tim shouted into the microphone, 'There's a bomb! Get out! Go on! Get out!'

Still no one ran towards the exit or made any effort to escape. They just sat there in stunned silence, not knowing what to think or do.

Tim shouted even louder. 'A BOMB! A BOMB!' His amplified voice boomed around the court. 'THERE IS A BOMB UNDER THIS COURT!'

A few spectators put their hands over their ears.

Mrs Malt put her hands over her eyes. Her cheeks had turned bright pink. She'd never felt so embarrassed in her life.

But no one left their seats.

Tim couldn't understand it. What was wrong?

Were they all mad? Or suicidal? Didn't they want to live?

'There's a bomb,' he said once more, his voice quieter and more hopeless, no longer believing that he could save the thousands of people crammed into the court. 'Don't you know what that means? In five minutes, you're all going to be blown up!'

No one moved. No one spoke. No one even picked up their coats or their umbrellas. They just sat in their seats, some smiling, others looking puzzled, a few drinking water or chewing snacks, and all of them watching Tim as if he was part of the show.

Tim looked across the court at Max.

On Max's face, Tim could see a mixture of amazement and horror.

This was one of the most important days of Max's life.

And Tim had ruined it.

Not bothering to shout, not caring who heard him apart from Max, Tim said, 'It's true. I promise it is, Max. There's a bomb under the court. It's going to go off in five minutes. If they don't leave now, they're all going to be killed. Why don't they believe me?'

Max didn't even need to think.

He knew that Tim would never lie about something so important. If Tim said there was a bomb, then there was a bomb.

Dropping his racket on the ground, Max ran to the side of the court where Natascha was sitting with the Malts. 'Get out! There's a bomb! Run! Run! You have to run! If you're still here in five minutes, you'll be blown up!'

Natascha jumped to her feet. She clapped her hands at Krishnan, Karishma and the Malts. 'Come on,' she said. 'Let's go! Didn't you hear him? There's a bomb!'

For a second, no one moved. All of them seemed to be paralysed by indecision. And then everyone moved at once. All around the court, people sprinted towards the exits.

A moment ago, no one had believed that a bomb could possibly have been placed under their seats. Now, everyone was sure that they only had a few seconds to save their lives.

Chapter 40

People poured out of the New Delhi Lawn Tennis Club, shouting and screaming, pushing and shoving, trying to get as far as possible from the bomb. They streamed into the street and ran in every direction.

Several taxis were waiting outside the tennis courts. They filled up immediately and then emptied just as fast. The streets were so full that the taxis couldn't drive anywhere.

The Malts and the Raffifis hurried as fast as anyone else, accompanied by Karishma and Krishnan.

They emerged through the tall iron gates of the New Delhi Lawn Tennis Club and dodged past the sign banning dogs from the club.

Mr Malt turned his head, looking up and down the street. He said, 'Does anyone know how to get back to the hotel?'

'I think it's that way,' said Mrs Malt, pointing to the left.

Max pointed to the right. 'I thought it was down there.'

'Please, come this way,' said Krishnan. 'I will show you to your hotel. Follow me! This way!'

He walked straight forward, but didn't manage to take more than three paces before his path was blocked by a small man in an elegant black suit.

'Excuse me, sir,' said Krishnan. 'May I come past?'

'No, you may not,' said Vijay Ghat as he stepped

forward, shoving Krishnan aside as if he hadn't even noticed the boy, and glared at Tim. 'Young man,' said Vijay Ghat in a stern voice, 'I hope you are very, very rich.'

'Why?' said Tim.

'Because I'm going to sue you for a million dollars.'

'I don't have a million dollars,' said Tim. 'I don't think I've even got ten dollars.'

'Then you will suffer the fate of anyone who doesn't pay his debts. You will spend many, many years in prison. And I hope no one comes to visit you.'

'But I've just saved all these people!'

'You haven't saved anyone,' interrupted Vijay Ghat. 'Your stupid joke has destroyed the final of the Vijay Ghat International Lawn Tennis Association Under-Sixteen Championship.'

'It's not a joke,' protested Tim.

'Don't try to deny what you've done,' said Vijay Ghat. 'You have ruined my tennis tournament! Years of my life have gone into this! And millions of rupees! They have been wasted! Wasted! All wasted! Young man, I shall sue you for every rupee that you own! I shall make your life a misery! I shall—'

But no one heard what else Vijay Ghat was going to do. His words were drowned out by an enormous roar.

White light flashed across the sky.

A wave of heat spread in every direction, scorching grass and clothes and hair and skin.

In the middle of the tennis club, precisely in the place where several thousand spectators had just been sitting, a huge ball of smoke rose in the air.

Chapter 41

The explosion could be heard for miles.

Wreckage was flung in every direction. Broken bricks, glass splinters and clumps of turf spewed across the city. Half a mile away, a shower of smouldering tennis balls rained down in the middle of a crowded street.

Houses were rocked and windows shattered. In shops and offices, people staggered backwards, grabbing the walls for support. No one knew what had happened. Was that an earthquake? Had a plane crashed into the city? Or was this the end of the world?

As the smoke cleared, and the emergency services arrived, the scale of devastation became apparent. Roofs and walls had crashed to the ground. Three buildings had collapsed. The courts and stands had been vaporised. Nothing remained of the New Delhi Lawn Tennis Club except two tall iron gates.

There was only one possible outcome for the Vijay Ghat International Lawn Tennis Association Under-Sixteen Championship. It was cancelled immediately. The final would never be finished. If Vilayati Jeera and Max Raffifi wanted to discover which of them was the better player, they would have to play another game. This year, the Vijay Ghat International Lawn Tennis Association Under-Sixteen Championship was not going to have a winner.

Vijay Ghat didn't mind. At least he was alive.

Only one person died in the explosion.

When the bomb blew up, the old woman was still searching through the tennis court, looking for her blue rat. She knew the timer was ticking down to zero, but she refused to leave the club without it.

The police found her body buried under a pile of bricks.

The blue rat had disappeared.

Perhaps it was killed in the explosion. Or perhaps it survived. Perhaps it sneaked down some drains or wriggled through a hole in a wall and escaped from the tennis club before the bomb went off. Perhaps it joined a gang of other rats and is still living on the streets of Delhi.

But none of that matters.

Whether the blue rat is dead or alive, it has lost its power. Now, no one is scared of it. No one believes that it is a god. And, most importantly, no one will ever again have to give up their children to the blue rat gang.

Chapter 42

A month after the explosion, Tim returned to the Taj Mahal.

He was accompanied by Mr Malt, Mrs Malt, Max and Natascha. Grk lay on the floor under their table.

As soon as they sat down, Mrs Malt said, 'Let's write the postcards now. Before the food arrives and everything gets mucky.' She reached into her handbag, pulled out three postcards and three black pens, and passed them to the children.

Tim, Natascha and Max hunched over the postcards and wrote to Krishnan and Karishma. There was no other way to communicate with them. Although their village had electricity now, they still didn't have phones or computers. They couldn't read or write, but there was one man in their village who could. If they received any letters, he would read them aloud. If they wanted to reply, he would write down whatever they wanted to say.

'Dear Krishnan and Karishma,' wrote Tim. 'I hope you're having a nice time with your mum and your dad and your sisters and your brothers. When are you coming to visit us in London? Soon, I hope. Love from Tim.'

Tim had just scrawled his signature when the waiter came to the table, carrying a notebook and a pen. 'Good evening. Hello, everybody. Welcome to the Taj Mahal. Are you ready to order?'

'I am,' said Tim, pushing aside his postcard. He was starving.

'Very good, sir,' said the waiter. 'What would you like?'

'Chicken korma, please. And some pilau rice. And a chapatti.'

'Excellent choice, sir.' The waiter smiled, then turned to Natascha. 'And for you, madam?'

While the waiter was taking everyone else's orders, Tim looked around the room, staring at the photographs on the walls and the diners at the other tables, and remembered why the Taj Mahal was his favourite restaurant in the whole world. He'd never been anywhere nicer. The waiters were friendly. The chicken korma was delicious. And, best of all, it was only fifteen minutes' walk from his house.

Tim had been to two Taj Mahals.

One was a big white building in India. The other was a restaurant near his home.

Some people said the Taj Mahal in India was the most beautiful building in the world. Well, they were welcome to it. Given the choice between the two Taj Mahals, Tim knew where he would rather be.

He settled back in his chair, took a sip of fizzy water and waited for his chicken korma to arrive.